'It's just...it' **night. I th** **killed when ** **flames...'**

Suddenly tears began to pour down her face. His arms went round her and he held her to him, soothing her with murmured words. 'Now, now—don't worry, sweetheart. This is just a reaction to the shock of the evening— just relax now.'

Gradually she became calmer, and she relaxed against Ronan, feeling the steady throb of his heart beating against hers. Then she wound her arms around him and pulled his head down, brushing her lips against his firm mouth.

'Thank you,' she whispered. 'This is just what I need.'

He gave a shudder, his clear blue eyes questioning hers. 'You're not making it easy to resist you, Lisa,' he said softly. 'Is this part of the treatment for shattered nerves?'

She laughed shakily. 'It could help...'

Judy Campbell is from Cheshire. As a teenager she spent a great year at high school in Oregon, USA, as an exchange student. She has worked in a variety of jobs, including teaching young children, being a secretary and running a small family business. Her husband comes from a medical family, and one of their three grown-up children is a GP. Any spare time— when she's not writing romantic fiction—is spent playing golf, especially in the Highlands of Scotland.

THE PREGNANT GP

BY
JUDY CAMPBELL

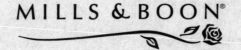

All the characters in this book have no existence outside the imagination of the author, and have no relation whatsoever to anyone bearing the same name or names. They are not even distantly inspired by any individual known or unknown to the author, and all the incidents are pure invention.

First published in Great Britain 2006
Harlequin Mills & Boon Limited,
Eton House, 18-24 Paradise Road, Richmond, Surrey TW9 1SR

© Judy Campbell 2006

ISBN 0 263 84709 8

Set in Times Roman 10½ on 13 pt.
03-0106-51384

Printed and bound in Spain
by Litografia Rosés, S.A., Barcelona

CHAPTER ONE

THE pain in Lisa Balfour's side had been a dull ache since the morning—now it seemed more intense, like a hot needle giving her occasional little stabs. It was just her luck that it should happen when she was in the middle of an interview, trying to appear bright, competent and exactly the sort of doctor Dr Ronan Gillespie wanted in his practice! She leaned forward slightly, trying to blank the pain out of her mind and concentrate on the questions he was asking her.

'What led you to apply for a job here in Arrandale?' Dr Gillespie asked, a pleasant Scottish lilt in his voice. He glanced down at her CV before him on the desk. 'You've been with a large practice in a thriving area—why change to a small practice in this remote place? There are vacancies in large medical centres in the bigger towns near here.'

Lisa took a deep breath as the stabbing pains subsided and said earnestly, 'I liked the idea of a smaller partnership, and I'd been wanting to move for some time…' A slight understatement. The fact was, she'd been *desperate* to move after the turmoil of life in Grangeford! 'I do have connections with Arrandale, because my mother came from here and loved it—although she never came back after she'd moved to

England. As my mother has died, it seems the right time to make a change.'

That was only partly the truth, but she wasn't going to tell Dr Gillespie the main reasons she'd chosen to come to this out-of-the-way place—they were too personal and distressing, things she wanted to keep to herself. And she could hardly reveal that because of what had happened in Grangeford she never wanted to set foot in the place again—wanted to block out any memories of her life there.

Dr Gillespie looked at her with polite interest. 'She never brought you here to see her childhood home?'

'No—my mother didn't seem very keen to revisit her past.' And with good reason, too, thought Lisa sadly. 'Now she's gone—well, I'd like to know more about the place she grew up in and loved so much…'

Her voice trailed off—it wasn't the time to go into her family history. If Dr Gillespie was surprised that she'd never visited Arrandale before, he gave no sign of it.

'It must have been a hard time for you,' he said quietly, 'but there's no doubt about it, if it's a new start you're after, you've chosen the right place. The countryside round Arrandale is very beautiful—I dare say it can compare favourably to anywhere in the world.'

'It seems so lovely and peaceful round here,' agreed Lisa. 'A complete contrast to the practice in Grangeford—that was frantically busy.'

He frowned slightly and gave an impatient sigh. 'It may not be the quiet option you and other people seem to imagine. I assure you we have the same problems here as in inner cities—perhaps not in such quantity. There are drug and alcohol issues here, as anywhere else. If you're looking for an easy life, don't seek it here, please.'

'Of course I didn't mean that I thought work here would be easy,' protested Lisa, stung by his suggested criticism. 'And I'm certainly not afraid of hard work…'

He nodded rather dismissively. Damn, she thought crossly, now I've given him the wrong impression. He'll think I'm just after a cushy number, whereas what I truly want is to be kept busy in a job I love—so busy that I can forget everything that has gone before.

'You see,' continued Dr Gillespie, 'my partner in the practice, Terry Newman, was involved in a skiing accident recently and has had complications following a very bad break in his leg—he'll be off work for a while yet. We'd already been thinking of taking on an extra salaried partner anyway as the patient list is really too big for two people—you can guess what it's like at the moment, with only me here.'

'It must be very difficult.'

The nagging little pain in her stomach stirred again and Lisa was grateful when the phone on his desk began ringing and shifted his attention. She could see a reflection of herself in a mirror on the opposite wall and was shocked at her appearance—a dead white face and rather sunken eyes with dark shadows under them stared back at her, and her normally buoyant honey-coloured hair lay lankly against her face. She didn't look as if she could do an hour's work, let alone a full day!

'Excuse me,' Dr Gillespie said as he picked up the phone. 'I'm sorry about this—it's probably an update on the condition of a patient from the community nurse.'

He answered the call, walking round the room as he talked. Lisa flicked a covert look at his tall and rangy figure—obviously he was a man who wouldn't suffer fools gladly, and yet there was something rather attractive about his assured manner. The cynical thought flew into her mind that he was just the kind of doctor that every woman patient would be a little in love with—that combination of good looks and authority could be very seductive in a man. He had the kind of poised, self-confident bearing of someone who had been to a public school and been taught how to conduct himself well.

Dr Gillespie bent over the desk, making a few notes, and Lisa turned her attention to the room. It was rather shabby and in need of decoration, but the window looked out on a wonderful view of woods and hills, with little farms nestling in the dales beyond the small town—it would be fun, exploring the area.

He put the phone down and gave an apologetic grimace. 'Hard to get away from this job even on a Saturday afternoon—as you'll know yourself. And now,' he added in a businesslike way, 'are there any questions you'd like to ask?'

There was an underlying briskness to his tone, the narrow intelligent face not giving too much away—rather aloof, in fact, a man not to be distracted from the matter in hand. He looked at her with eyes of a quite startling blue, and she noticed an intriguing little scar slightly puckering the side of his cheek.

'How many patients are registered here?' she asked.

'About four thousand—but we do have a large area to cover. Again, this can be very demanding.' He said this with slight emphasis, as if to underline his point about hard work. 'There are several villages around who use us, and a small cottage hospital about five miles away, which is useful for minor ops and recuperation, otherwise we have to go to Inverleith.'

Lisa nodded, aware that he was underscoring how busy the practice was. Probably Ronan Gillespie would be a hard taskmaster and she suspected he had a short fuse, but she could handle that as long as he was dependable and had a sense of humour behind that serious expression. If only he'd give her a chance and believe her when she said she didn't mind hard work! It would be a change from her last job where the days had become an ordeal, and she'd woken up every morning with a sense of dread at the day ahead.

Another stab of pain pierced her on the right side of her abdomen and snaked round her back, making her feel nauseous and slightly faint. Damn! Lisa swallowed hard and focussed her attention on the serious deep blue eyes looking at her across the desk. She wished she hadn't had the prawns last night—they'd seemed so delicious at the time. Ridiculous timing to get food poisoning just when she wanted to appear alert and impressive. She gave a little gasp as a more powerful pain gripped her insides and the room became slightly blurred.

Dr Gillespie looked at her sharply, frowning. 'You feeling OK? You're a little pale.'

Lisa stretched her mouth in a mirthless smile. She might feel she was going to die at any minute but she didn't want him to know it.

'Fine…not bad at all,' she said brightly, digging her nails into her palms to take her mind off the things her stomach was doing. If she could just get this interview over with, she'd think about how ill she was afterwards. She really wanted this job. If she lived here she could find out more about the place where her mother had grown up and imagine what her childhood had been like. It was this that had given her the impetus she'd needed to leave Grangeford and turn her back on the complications of life there.

Dr Gillespie glanced keenly at her again as if not fully satisfied, then resumed after a few seconds, 'How do you feel about being on call some nights? Although we do have an arrangement with an outside agency to do most of the weekend calls, we still do some weekdays—hopefully we'll get full cover in time. I imagine you have agency help at your present practice?'

He observed her questioningly, then smiled, the scar creasing into a dimple, giving him a certain rakish air, turning a handsome face into an interesting one.

'And of course,' he added, 'this building isn't exactly state of the art…not really suitable for a medical centre. We keep hoping something will miraculously turn up, but anything that's any good is way above budget.'

He seems to be doing his best to put me off, thought Lisa. Perhaps he's trying to tell me he doesn't think I'm up to the job.

She shrugged. 'Doing night calls doesn't bother me—as long as there aren't too many nights a month. And although purpose-built buildings are nice, a good practice doesn't rely on that alone.'

Ronan Gillespie nodded. 'I agree—but I really need someone soon. Locums aren't proving too satisfactory. How much notice do you have to give to your present practice?'

'I've already left,' said Lisa.

He looked at her in surprise, eyebrows lifted questioningly.

She interjected rather too quickly, too smoothly, 'During my mother's illness I wanted to be with her and so I left some weeks ago, just helping them out with locum work.'

Again—not the whole truth, but more or less accurate. This time Dr Gillespie eyed her more thoughtfully as if he'd glimpsed more behind her words than she was revealing.

'So you could start immediately?'

'Yes—as soon as you like. Aagh!'

She couldn't help giving a yelp of agony as the pain really

kicked in. She doubled up, clutching her stomach, and Dr Gillespie gave an exclamation of concern, bounding round the desk and putting his arm round her.

'Good God—what's wrong? Have you got cramps?'

The room danced before Lisa's eyes and with a peculiar sense of oblivion she slid off the chair and drifted into a world dominated by the paralysing pain in her side. Vaguely she heard Dr Gillespie's voice coming from a long way off, then felt herself being lifted up and put down gently onto a bed. Even through her agony it felt very comforting—she knew she was in competent hands.

'Tell me where it hurts, Lisa—here? Lower right-hand side of your abdomen and round the side?'

He probed gently, and she gave a gasp as even that gentle pressure sent waves of knife-like electric shocks radiating through her body. 'Don't do that,' she moaned. 'I feel terrible. Don't touch me, please…'

His voice was calm and soothing. 'Now, don't you worry yourself—we'll have you sorted out in no time. There'll be an ambulance on its way very soon…'

'Ambulance?' she questioned faintly. 'But I'm in the middle of an interview… I think it must be food poisoning.'

Lisa made an attempt to sit up then collapsed back, defeated. What was the good of protesting? She felt too terrible to put on any pretence. She wanted this job but it looked as if it was going to slip from her grasp.

Dr Gillespie gave a dry laugh. 'We'll give the interview a miss today…one thing at a time, eh? And as for food poisoning, Dr Balfour, I'm not so sure about that diagnosis.'

Then there was a blur of people in fluorescent coats filling the room, the odd sensation of being completely powerless as she was carried out to the ambulance and the uncomfortable ride to the hospital with an oxygen mask clamped over her face. Through the waves of pain was the sense of disappointment that she could say goodbye to this particular job, mixed with the embarrassment of her position and a funny feeling of loss that she wouldn't be working with Dr Ronan Gillespie after all.

Ronan watched the ambulance wind down the hill towards Inverleith, then turned moodily back towards the surgery. He'd suspected that Lisa hadn't been feeling well—she'd looked as white as a ghost. And wasn't it just his luck that the only suitable candidate for the job should collapse on him just as he'd decided that he needed to look no further? He didn't entirely believe that the sole reason Lisa wanted to come to Arrandale was to find out about her mother's childhood home, but there was something gutsy about the way she'd struggled through the interview when she must have been feeling terrible that had impressed him. Perhaps he'd be taking a gamble, offering her the job, but instinctively he felt she was not the sort of colleague to let you down.

He sighed. Lisa was an attractive girl—darned attractive, the kind of girl that he would have gone for two or three years ago. He gave a hollow laugh. He'd learned his lesson where romance was concerned, and it would be a long long time before he would be tempted to think of any kind of commitment again. That was why it had been such a shock to feel the most extraordinary flicker of attraction when he'd gathered Lisa in his arms and placed her on the examining couch after she'd fainted—after all, he'd only met the girl half an hour before!

Returning to his room, Ronan sat down at his desk feeling shaken and irritated. What the hell had happened to him just then? It was as if a switch had been turned on and he'd become intensely aware of a woman's looks for the first time in ages. It was damned ridiculous and quite out of character. He gazed moodily out of the window and told himself sternly that he was only interested in the woman from a work point of view— someone who would be a reliable partner and shift some of the ever-increasing burden of work from his shoulders.

He put his head in his hands wearily. Perhaps he was going mad through overwork, his brain too tired to concentrate on merely interviewing someone. He'd allowed himself to drop his guard and view her as a girl with a lovely face and a knock-out figure, rather than as a future colleague. If he was going to take on Lisa Balfour as a partner, he'd have to be much more objective than that!

The flowers by Lisa's bed had a fresh spring-like smell—just a dainty bunch of daffodils, but they were beautiful and some-how uplifting. Lisa wondered who had sent them—she didn't know anyone in this area. She sighed and closed her eyes. If only the appendicitis had held off for a few more hours until she'd finished the interview. If Dr Gillespie had offered her the job, he surely wouldn't have then reneged on his offer because she was ill. Fat chance she had of getting the position now. There must have been other applicants—probably, she thought gloomily, all healthy, strapping people able to start immediately.

'So how is the patient, then? Feeling a little more human?'

Lisa gave a jump and opened her eyes. Ronan Gillespie was standing at the bottom of the bed, his blue eyes looking down at her questioningly.

'A lot better,' Lisa smiled ruefully. 'I…I'm so sorry about putting you to all that bother…'

'Don't think another thing about it. The main thing is we got you to hospital in time and they diagnosed the problem pretty quickly.' He gave an unexpected smile that suddenly made him look more boyish and less aloof and he said teasingly, 'I think you were just testing out the facilities of the cottage hospital I told you about. Are you in much pain?'

'Not bad at all. They did a laparoscopy, thank goodness, so I'll be out soon.'

He nodded approvingly. 'Ah, yes—this minimal invasive surgery is fantastic—a far cry from our parents' day. David Grieves told me he'd do that if possible. It sounds as if the appendix wasn't too badly infected—he wouldn't have risked the spread of contamination through a small incision. How long had you been feeling ill?'

'I'd had a vague feeling of discomfort for a few days,' admitted Lisa. 'But I thought it was the prawns I'd eaten the day before the interview that had caused the problem. With hindsight I obviously had a grumbling appendix.'

'You certainly look much better than you did,' he observed.

It depended on what he meant by 'better', thought Lisa despondently, horribly aware that her hair was a tangled mass and she probably looked as white as the hospital gown she was wearing. Ronan Gillespie was the kind of man who made you want to look your best—not like a pathetic waif. It had been kind of him to come and she was grateful that he'd reacted quickly when she'd collapsed. But now she wanted him to go, allow her to wallow in self-pity at her weak state and the fact that she still needed to get a job.

A young woman in white trousers and tunic walked up to Ronan. She smiled at Lisa. 'Excuse me for butting in, do you mind if I have a quick word with Dr Gillespie?'

Ronan nodded at the newcomer. 'Ah, Tanya, there you are. Dr Balfour, let me introduce my sister, Tanya, who's just finishing as a physio here before she goes to Italy for six months on a sort of exchange with a hospital there. Tanya, this is Dr Lisa Balfour—I'm hoping she'll be joining me at the practice in the near future, when she's got over the loss of her appendix.'

Tanya came forward and took Lisa's hand. 'That's great news. Ronan's had a torrid time, trying to keep the place going while his partner's laid up.'

Lisa gaped at them both in surprise. 'Do you mean I've got the job? But you needed someone to start immediately. I thought I'd blown it when I collapsed on you.'

Dr Gillespie gave a grimace. 'I can limp along until you've recovered—but certainly I'm offering you the job.' He looked at her reflectively but his voice was forceful. 'You do understand that I expect 100 per cent commitment in a very busy practice?'

'Of course. As I told you before, I'm not afraid of hard work.'

Tanya chuckled. 'Then you'll fit in very well with my brother—he lives and breathes his practice!'

His smile was rueful. 'I haven't had much time to do anything else. To be honest, very few people seem to want the job! Not that I wouldn't have chosen you—it's just that when people are crying out for GPs, a practice like mine in the back of beyond isn't everyone's first choice.'

'A smaller practice appeals to me. Makes life less complicated.'

'I see. I'll try and keep things as simple as possible, then! I take it you want the job?'

Lisa laughed. 'Why, yes…yes, I'd like to accept and I'm sure I'll be able to start fairly soon. Thank you Dr Gillespie.'

'Don't start till your surgeon tells you it's OK, however much my brother needs you,' said Tanya sternly.

'Tanya's right—and if we're to be colleagues, I think you could start calling me by my first name! By the way, is there anything we can do to help? Have you any personal belongings we can get for you from your hotel?'

'That's very kind. I was just staying for two nights at the small hotel in the village—Birsk Lodge—and I do have a bag of overnight things there. I'll go back to recuperate for a few days at the Lodge and I'll get my things sent on from Grangeford.'

Tanya made a face and looked at her brother. 'You can't let the poor girl convalesce at Birsk Lodge—it's absolutely ghastly! Terribly gloomy and depressing. After a few days there she'll go into a decline.'

She turned impulsively to Lisa. 'I've got a marvellous idea—you must stay at The Rowans where Ronan and I live. It's a huge place, and we've got a sort of daily help-cum-housekeeper who won't mind looking after you—isn't that right, Ronan?'

Lisa flicked an embarrassed glance at Ronan. He certainly didn't look very pleased with his sister's marvellous idea—just the opposite. His expression was stony, his blue eyes rather flinty.

'Of course,' he said politely, stretching his mouth into a stiff smile that didn't reach his eyes. 'You would be most welcome.'

'I couldn't possibly do that,' Lisa protested swiftly and firmly. 'I'll be absolutely fine at Birsk Lodge, and I'm sure I'll find a place to rent or buy very soon.'

'Then you'll only need to spend a short time at The Rowans in that case. I'm right, aren't I, Ronan? Lisa would be no trouble at all, and if it helps to get her better more quickly, then it has to be the right thing!'

Ronan nodded with every evidence of reluctance. 'Tanya's right—you wouldn't be doing yourself any favours staying at Birsk Lodge.'

Tanya clapped her hands and smiled delightedly. 'That's fixed, then! When you're allowed out of here, you're to go straight to The Rowans and no argument!'

Suddenly Lisa felt too tired to argue. After all, the hotel *was* pretty awful and surely it wouldn't take her long to find somewhere to rent even if she couldn't buy a property.

'Thank you. If you're sure, it would be lovely to stay for a few days.'

'Good,' said Ronan heavily. 'I'll speak to David Grieves and find out when you're going to be discharged and get a bed made up.'

His face had that serious look she'd become used to at her interview, blue eyes looking gravely into hers, then he gave a half-wave as he turned round and strode back through the small ward with his sister, who said smilingly over her shoulder, 'I'll see you before I go, Lisa. Good to meet you.'

Lisa lay back on her pillow, a surge of relief flowing through her. Thank God she'd no need to look for another job. She hadn't realised how much she'd wanted this one until she'd thought she'd blown it. She was surprised at the buzz of excitement she felt at the thought of working with Ronan. For heaven's sake, he was just an ordinary GP, wasn't he? His direct manner could be disconcerting but she felt if she gave it her best shot they would get on well enough. She just hoped she hadn't done the wrong thing by accepting his offer of hospitality—although it had been much more his sister's offer than his!

'Is Dr Gillespie your GP, then?' asked the pretty young nurse who took her blood pressure a few minutes later.

'I'm about to become his colleague when I get out of here,' replied Lisa. 'He came to tell me I'd got the job he'd interviewed me for.'

'Lucky you!' sighed the girl. 'I think he's gorgeous, and madly eligible, too.'

'I'm surprised he's not married or going out with anyone,' remarked Lisa. 'He must be well into his thirties.'

'He's pretty elusive and hard to get to know—quite a few of my friends have been after him, but they've never got anywhere. He was engaged for a while, but it all came to grief — I don't know why.' The nurse tucked the sphygmomanometer back in its box and added, 'He hasn't had a girlfriend since. Still…' she winked '…one can always live in hope!'

She grinned at Lisa and swung off to the next bed.

It was an intriguing thought that a man with no shortage of females wanting to throw themselves at him should stay with the memory of a love from long ago. Perhaps that was why he looked so serious, mused Lisa. She guessed that he didn't put aside much time for play.

She turned to look at the note left on the bunch of daffodils by her bed. It said, 'I've never interviewed anyone before with an acute appendicitis. Get well soon, Ronan Gillespie.'

Now, that was rather astonishing, reflected Lisa. She would never have believed that behind his efficient brusque manner lurked such a thoughtful man! Her feelings were tinged with a curious interest at the thought of working with someone who kept himself to himself. It seemed he'd had an unhappy and mysterious past—but didn't most people have ghosts in their backgrounds, events that had helped to shape the people they were today?

Ronan stood in the car park and looked back at the hospital for a minute before getting into his car.

'I can't believe I just asked Lisa Balfour to stay with me— I must be mad,' he muttered irritably to himself as he opened the car door. 'Why the hell did I allow Tanya to bulldoze me into doing such a thing?'

He could picture the ripples of gossip there'd be in the practice when an attractive single girl like her was lodging with him. He imagined the tongues wagging, saying that it was about time 'poor Dr Gillespie met someone' and how suitable Lisa Balfour would be. Perhaps deep down he was frightened of starting a relationship again, or putting himself into an embarrassing position after the hassle he'd been through with Maisie. He shuddered slightly, remembering the threats she'd hurled at him when they'd parted. He only hoped that they'd never see each other again.

He changed gear more aggressively than he should as he rounded the corner at the bottom of the hill. Best not to dwell on the nightmare of the past. He had to look forward, and now he hoped he'd found someone in Lisa with experience and a sense of commitment who actually wanted to work in a remote practice in a dilapidated building. Perhaps he'd be able to relax a little, play some golf and go fishing, visit his mother in Glasgow and get some kind of a life of his own—anything rather than allow his life and Lisa's to cross except in the matter of work!

He parked the car in the driveway of the attractive old

house, built in the uncompromising granite of the area and softened by the spread of ivy over the walls, and got out. He stretched his long limbs and gazed down the valley at the reddening evening sky. Whatever the true story was behind Lisa's decision to move to Arrandale, he was happy to take her on. But he'd keep his distance. There would be no socialising after work—everything would be businesslike. He opened the front door and scooped up his morning post, gazing at it unseeingly for a minute, Lisa's image floating into his mind.

'I'll just have to be very careful I don't mix business with pleasure this time,' he murmured.

A large sheepdog tore out of the kitchen and flung itself on him in an ecstasy of welcome, barking frantically.

'Hello, Tam.' Ronan ruffled the dog's head affectionately. 'You may be in line for some more walks with me now—I've got some help at last. I'll just have to hope that I've learned my lesson where women are concerned eh?'

Tam pricked up his ears at the mention of the word 'walk' and ran to the door, looking back at his master hopefully. Ronan laughed.

'Come on, then, old boy. Let's go and drink a toast to Dr Lisa Balfour. May we have a long and happy business relationship!'

CHAPTER TWO

THE bedroom was spacious and airy with a beautiful bay window looking out over fields and a flash of blue loch beyond. A large double bed with carved posts and a matching wardrobe with a long mirror and a small desk beside it faced the window, and Lisa could imagine a maid in Victorian times coming to light a fire in the morning in the pretty fireplace surrounded by blue and white tiles. It was clear that Ronan came from a different world from hers—an opulent background where wealth, education and privilege were the norm. No worries about scraping together the money for medical school fees or paying for board and lodging when doing an elective course. Compared to her, she thought cynically, he'd had it easy!

There was a cavernous bathroom next door so that it was like her own private suite, right at the other end of a corridor from Ronan. And that was fortunate because she had the feeling that Ronan seemed very anxious to keep her at arm's length while she was staying with him. It was horribly clear to Lisa that if his sister hadn't suggested that she stay for a short while, he certainly would never have done so!

Lisa was very grateful to him for his hospitality but after

nearly a week she felt she knew no more about Ronan than she had at the start—even though they'd had supper together the night before.

Most nights Lisa had eaten by herself, Ronan coming in too late from surgery or out at meetings. Tanya had departed to Italy the day after they'd met, and now Ronan and Lisa were sitting like a Victorian couple at either end of a large table. Betty, his housekeeper, had left a delicious-smelling venison casserole, which Lisa doled out between them.

'Betty's a wonderful cook,' she volunteered after they'd sat in silence for a few minutes. 'I'm eating far too much—I'll be getting as fat as a barrel.'

Blue eyes studied her across the table and for some reason Lisa felt her heart start to thump at his inspection.

'You look a hundred per cent better than you did at your interview,' he observed shortly. 'There's some colour in your cheeks and you've lost those hollows under your eyes. About time you got your appetite back.'

He resumed eating and Lisa sighed. Was he always going to be such hard work? She'd sensed a more approachable side to him when he'd visited her in the hospital and offered her a job, but now she was staying in his house he was clearly petrified that she would take advantage of him in some way. She'd put him out of his misery!

'While I've been recuperating,' she said, 'I've been look-ing at some properties in the area. There's a little cottage I'd like to buy but at the moment it's only for rent.'

'In the village?'

'No—it's by the loch and it has a tiny garden that I think I could manage. The owner's going abroad. Do you know him—Bill Garrity?'

Ronan nodded. 'He's a wildlife photographer. He's taken some spectacular pictures of the local birds.' He paused for a second then said lightly, 'And when would you be going?'

'Possibly next weekend. I start work tomorrow, of course, but I've nothing much to take with me, so I could go on Saturday morning—if you could stand me for another five days!'

He smiled courteously at her. 'You're very welcome to stay as long as you want, although I'm sure you want your own place. I'll help you with your stuff on Saturday.'

Lisa smiled to herself. She thought she'd detected a distinct note of relief in his voice! She leaned back in her chair and, emboldened by the excellent red wine he'd offered her, looked at him with an impish grin.

'This is a beautiful house, but don't you ever feel you're rattling round in it, especially now your sister's gone abroad?'

Ronan shrugged. 'It's belonged to the family for generations, and of course it is far too big for my sister and I, but we're desperate to hang onto it because we love it so much. I did think of getting somewhere smaller…' He paused for a second and swirled his wine round in his glass, watching the light glinting on the liquid, then looked up and smiled. 'Never had time to look around, I suppose, and, truth to tell, I don't think I could live in a small place—I've grown used to having space around me!'

Lisa reflected on the flat she and her mother had lived in—you could have fitted the whole place into his drawing room! Ronan had been brought up in a different world from hers, that was plain. He got up and refilled her glass and then his own.

'What about you—have you a house in Grangeford?'

'I've a flat I put on the market, and my mother lived in a council flat, so there's nothing to sell there. In fact, I don't think I'll leave much trace of myself or my family now I've moved up here.'

'You've no regrets about leaving Grangeford?'

Lisa gave a hollow laugh. 'None at all. I intend to look forward. I want to forget the past.'

Ronan raised his eyebrows and looked at her assessingly. 'So you're running away from unhappy memories?'

She flushed. 'I prefer to call it shutting a door on one part of my life and opening another.' She looked at him challengingly. 'I imagine all of us have things we want to put behind us.'

He took a long sip of wine, then frowned and said tersely, 'You're right, it's very good advice—best to look forward. Let's hope you find that new start here.' He stood up abruptly and drew the heavy velvet curtains across the long windows.

I guess the broken engagement still hurts, thought Lisa. He's probably never got over it. She leant back in her chair and finished the last drops of wine in her glass before leaving the room. She'd learned a little more about her new employer, but not much!

Ronan sat at the table for some time after she'd left and looked glumly at her empty seat. He couldn't deny that he was pleased that Lisa had found somewhere else to live—it was what he wanted, wasn't it? Having such an attractive woman living in the same house as him was unsettling, he couldn't concentrate at all. He'd found his thoughts straying when he was at a meeting, making excuses when everyone stayed for a drink afterwards, feeling that he should get home and see her before she went to bed. And he wasn't sleeping as well as he normally did…a very irritating state of affairs. So it was a good thing that she'd be moving out and he could be himself again, have his own space—a very good thing indeed.

* * *

It was her first day at work. Lisa opened one of the sash windows and leaned out, breathing in the fresh cool air of the early morning, the incisive call of a thrush nearby sounding like a wake-up call. It couldn't have been more different from Grangeford where there was always a slight whiff of fumes from the traffic on the main road, if not from the airport not so far away!

Ronan had already gone out on a call, so she would make her own way to the surgery. She popped her head round the door of the kitchen where Betty was vigorously scouring the old wooden table.

'See you later, Betty—wish me luck!'

'Aye. You'll need it—they're a right bunch of hypochondriacs!' was Betty's forthright reply.

Ronan was right about the practice being remote, thought Lisa as she got out of her car and gazed at the view spread before her. Her eyes marvelled at the panorama of a wide valley bounded by rolling hills that was the backdrop to Arrandale, the ruins of an old tower standing like a sentinel on the rise above the medical centre. The road snaked down the hill and in the early morning sunlight the place looked beautiful, glistening after a shower of rain. The little stone cottages gave way to a knot of shops and a gracious-looking church bounding a small square with a green sward of grass around it.

How sad that her mother had never come back to this beautiful place—never felt able to show Lisa where she'd spent her childhood, although Lisa knew the underlying reason. If only she'd been able to persuade her mother to forget the dramatic events that had led up to her leaving Arrandale when she'd been sixteen… Lisa shrugged her shoulders. It was all in the past now and at least she herself knew that her real roots lay in Arrandale and not in the suburban streets of Grangeford. And that was a good thing—fewer reminders of a place which she'd come to hate.

It looks so peaceful and well ordered, she thought. Hard to imagine anything like drugs or alcohol being a problem here.

The practice was the last house in the village: it had once been two farm cottages, now knocked together to make one. The brickwork needed pointing, the wood in the window-frames needed renewing and the fencing round the small car park was falling down. Perhaps running the practice on his own had meant Ronan had had no time to update the place— and that, reflected Lisa with satisfaction, was perhaps something she could organize. She would enjoy improving the look of the centre.

'Allow me!' A hand reached round her and pushed the door open. Ronan had come up the steps behind her. 'Welcome to The Coppice Medical Centre!'

He smiled down at her, his dark hair ruffled in the cold wind, his clear blue eyes meeting hers in a sudden lifting of his aloof nature.

'Come and meet Val and Cora Simmonds,' he said as they stepped into a small, stuffy and crowded waiting room, where curious eyes followed them and a hush descended as they walked through. 'They're my receptionists and the people that keep me sane in this madhouse!'

Two flushed round faces, looking remarkably alike, smiled at Lisa as she and Ronan entered the office behind Reception. The room was lined with shelves bulging with case notes and a computer in the corner bounced a graphic around its screen in perpetual motion. A coffee-percolator simmered on a work-top, its fresh aroma inviting.

'Hello, there, Dr Balfour—welcome to The Coppice!' One of the women stepped forward and grasped Lisa's hand enthusiastically. 'I'm Val Simmonds and this is Cora, my sister. I'm so glad you're recovered from your operation. That must have been really scary!'

Lisa wondered if she'd ever be able to tell them apart: they both had rosy faces framed by short curly hair and rather portly figures encased in tight navy-blue suits. They reminded her irresistibly of Tweedledum and Tweedledee.

Ronan raised an amused eyebrow at Lisa's expression. 'Don't worry, you'll soon know which is which. For a start, one of them is left-handed—but don't ask me if it's Cora or Val!'

The sisters smiled goodnaturedly and Val said, 'People always get us mixed up, but I'm taller than Cora—and, of course,' she added mischievously, 'much slimmer!'

Cora slapped Val lightly on her wrist, then said briskly, 'Enough of that! Now, Doctors, there's a full surgery this morning—all the emergency slots have been filled already, and there are several home visits to be made. Here's a list of this morning's patients so far. A cup of coffee to start with?'

'Just what I need,' stated Ronan. 'You can see how they bully me! I'll show you your room, Lisa—it's at the back and I'm across the corridor. I'm afraid you're being thrown in at the deep end, but if you need any help, just buzz me on the intercom and I'll come through. I think you'll find we have a lot of curious patients keen to meet you!'

Lisa's room was small but adequate, with a large window on one side covered by a blind, a rather battered desk in front of it and an old-fashioned carpet in a faded pattern covered the floor. An examining couch against one wall and a hand-basin under some cupboards completed the furnishings. She sat down at her desk and looked around at her new world—somewhat shabbier than her room in Grangeford, but somehow friendlier.

'And now for a fresh start,' she murmured as she pressed the button to activate the call system in Reception. She felt a sudden lifting of her spirits—it was good to be back at work and without the problems of the old practice niggling away at her every day.

The door was pushed open and an overweight man in his fifties came in, wearing a pair of oily dungarees. He sank to the chair like a large bear and leant over to shake her hand, starting to talk before she could even open her mouth.

'Pleased to meet you, Dr Balfour. I believe you've come to help Dr Gillespie. You've had a rough start, haven't you? Fell ill at the interview, I hear. What was the trouble?'

Lisa suppressed a smile—it felt as if there was slight role reversal here.

'News travels fast, doesn't it? I'm quite OK now, thank you—just had my appendix out, that's all!'

The man pursed his lips judiciously. 'That can be very nasty—my cousin was at death's door with that. You want to be careful not to overdo it—the effects of the op can take months to get over, you know.'

'I'm sure I'll be fine, Mr Berry. Now, how can I help you?' Lisa interrupted hastily. They were after all meant to be discussing his ailments, not hers!

The man sighed. 'I only hope you can—otherwise it's a divorce I'll be getting! Don't laugh but it's my snoring. My wife says the whole house shakes when I snore and she's moved into the spare room. I know it's a silly matter, but she made me come to see you. We've got her mother coming to stay so I need to sort it out before she comes!'

He was trying to make a joke of it, but Lisa knew that the problem could be infuriating for the patient's partner and test relationships to the limit. She looked at him assessingly—he was a huge man and probably excess weight was making it hard to breathe when he lay down.

'It isn't a silly matter for either of you,' she said. 'You did the right thing to come and see me. Snoring can be caused by something quite innocent like a soft palate or it can occasionally have a more serious underlying cause.'

Mr Berry looked slightly alarmed. 'I didn't know it could be serious—in what way?'

'In certain cases it could be a sign of coronary heart disease, or it may be that you suffer from sleep apnoea, where you have a temporary stop in breathing. I should like to run a few tests.'

'And will that tell us what's wrong?'

'This may sound bizarre, Mr Berry, but I'd really like your wife to tape-record your snoring—it could give me a few more clues as to the cause. Your airway may be obstructed in some way and it does occur in people who are overweight.'

Mr Berry grimaced. 'I know what you're going to say, doctor. I'm a bit hefty, aren't I?'

'It would help you to lose weight,' Lisa said gently, 'and I can give you a diet sheet to follow. Meanwhile, I'd like you to have some blood tests, which would show up anything untoward—tests for thyroid, liver function and cholesterol and a full blood count.'

Her patient looked impressed. 'All that just because I'm snoring?'

'As I said, snoring can be caused by a number of things—best to be on the safe side. Just losing some weight might help enormously, but there are other options as well.'

'I'm obliged, Doctor. I'm glad I came now. Thought you'd send me packing for being a fusspot.'

Lisa smiled. 'Not at all, Mr Berry. If you have any concerns about your health, you must come and see us.'

Mr Berry lumbered up to his feet. 'Well, I hope you'll settle up here OK.' He turned back as if with an afterthought. 'If you have any trouble with your car, let me know, I'll see you right. I run Berry's Garage in the village—Dr Gillespie uses me all the time!'

It was an interesting morning—a succession of patients from a baby of three months old to a ninety-year-old man who had hurt his back decorating his bedroom. Most of them were curious to meet the doctor who'd come to help Dr Gillespie and Lisa found herself answering the same questions over and over again.

'Are you going to join the practice?'

'Are you feeling better after your operation?'

She began to think she should have put up a notice by the door with the answers on!

Her last patient was a plump, middle-aged woman who limped in slowly.

'Mrs Glendinning, I believe?' said Lisa, consulting her list and bringing up the woman's name on the computer screen before her.

Mrs Glendinning's eyes were round with curiosity behind thick-lensed spectacles. She sat herself down opposite

Lisa and leaned forward eagerly, pouring out a torrent of words with the comments Lisa had come to expect that morning!

'We were all sorry to hear that you've been ill, Doctor—what a terrible way to start your time here! Have you fully recovered now?'

Was there anyone in Arrandale who didn't know she'd been ill?

'Thanks to the marvellous surgeon and the cottage hospital, I'm as good as new now!'

'That's a relief,' said Mrs Glendinning, looking slightly disappointed that Lisa hadn't revealed the exact nature of her operation. 'You'll be staying with us, then?'

'I've joined the practice, yes. It seems a lovely area.' Before the woman could slip in another question, Lisa said quickly, 'Now, what is the trouble, Mrs Glendinning?'

The woman's expression changed to one of gloom. 'I doubt you can help, Doctor—it's my feet. I'm in agony with them. Sometimes I feel they're on fire—I can hardly get to my work.'

'What do you do?'

A look of pride crossed Mrs Glendinning's face. 'I work at Glenside House—it's the big house in the woods overlooking the loch. It's owned by the laird, Sir Richard Carstairs. I keep it in good shape, do all the cleaning…'

Lisa's heart gave an extra beat and she looked up quickly, her eyes wide with surprise and a certain shock. She hadn't thought she'd come across the name Carstairs so soon. It was probably very commonplace in these parts, but it sent her heart racing, as it had done when her mother had first told her of her connections with an Arrandale family of that name.

'I beg your pardon? Did you say Carstairs?'

'That's right, Doctor. He's very particular that the house should be kept nice—it's been in his family for generations.'

Her mother's voice seemed to echo in her ears. 'The Carstairs in those days were very cruel —they would never have countenanced the scandal they thought I'd brought on them. I had no choice but to go along with what they said and leave the area, pregnant, alone and only sixteen, to have the baby in a home in Grangeford—well away from the tittle-tattle of local gossip.'

Whenever she thought about her mother's treatment by an unfeeling family, Lisa felt a shiver of sadness go through her. But it was mixed with pride—as a young woman with a child, her mother had coped magnificently, bringing her daughter up on her own, asking help from no one. The reasons for her mother's bitter attitude towards men and her insistence that Lisa should get a training at all costs were clear. But Lisa knew her mother had never stopped loving the place of her birth and that had given Lisa the impetus to come up to Arrandale. She even felt a little leap of happiness at the thought of getting to know more about her background over the next few months. She smiled sympathetically at her patient.

'Looking after a large house is very hard work—it must take a toll on your feet!'

'Aye, and I love the job, but I'm not doing it properly at the moment, and that's a fact. Sir Richard's a very nice man, but if he thinks I'm not up to it, he may get someone else— and there aren't many other jobs to be had in Arrandale.'

The woman's face wobbled for a moment, betraying the anxiety she felt, and Lisa said soothingly, 'Well, then, let me see if we can do something to help you, and find out what the trouble is.'

Mrs Glendinning's feet were red and swollen, with large cracks spreading from in between her toes. Lisa looked at them closely, noting how the angry-looking skin had begun to spread to her ankles, which looked puffy and pink.

'Those look very painful. How long have they been like this?'

'A few weeks,' admitted the woman. 'I kept thinking they'd get better—I bathed them in hot mustard and water every evening, but now they're so bad I can hardly get my shoes on. Do you think anything can be done about it?'

'I hope we can get them back to normal very soon,' said Lisa cheerfully, smiling at the look of relief which spread like a rainbow over Mrs Glendinning's worried face.

'What you've got is a very bad dose of athlete's foot,' continued Lisa. 'It probably started off rather itchy, but the cracks have allowed infection to get in over time—no wonder it's so painful. I can give you powder to apply and some antibiotics should get rid of the infection.'

The woman puffed out her cheeks and smiled. 'Is that all? Thank the Lord for that!'

'You need to take care of them,' warned Lisa. 'Because of the infection you must rest for at least two days, elevating the foot. If the infection spreads up your leg it could be serious.'

Mrs Glendinning looked at her, aghast. 'Rest for two days? I can't do that! Sir Richard's having a large party to stay at the house this weekend and I don't like to let him down—he's such a good employer…'

'I'll write a note for you,' reassured Lisa, impressed by her patient's loyalty to her boss. 'But I must emphasise it's most important for you to rest.'

'Right, Doctor,' sighed Mrs Glendinning. 'I'll do as you

say. Perhaps my daughter-in-law will help out—after all, I do my bit with babysitting.'

'That's a good idea. Come back next week and let me check on how it is—and make sure you use your own towel so as not to infect anyone else.'

Lisa wrote a quick note to the woman's employer and gave it to her. Painfully Mrs. Glendinning began to move across the room, turning when she got to the door.

'Thank you doctor—it's been very nice to meet you.' She gave a chuckle and looked mischievously at Lisa. 'We were all wondering what poor Dr Gillespie's new partner would be like—he's needed help for a long time now since Dr Newman had his accident. Someone young and attractive like you will do him all the good in the world! He hasn't had much fun over the past few years…'

That makes two of us, reflected Lisa wryly as she updated Mrs. Glendinning's notes. Perhaps it was time for both of them to start enjoying life!

Ronan put his head round the door after Mrs Glendinning had gone out. 'How about some coffee to revive you? And then perhaps you'd come with me on a few house visits— show you a little of the area.'

'That would be great,' said Lisa, standing up and stretching.

'I expect you've had a pretty good grilling from your patients. I see Arthur Berry was on your list—has he mentioned his garage yet?' he said with an amused smile.

'He has,' admitted Lisa, thinking how much more relaxed Ronan seemed at work than he did when they were together at home. 'But they were all very welcoming—when I could get a word in—and they all seemed to know I'd been ill!'

'New travels like lightning around here. I expect everyone

is relieved that they won't have to wait days to see me for non-urgent cases now you're here. Anything startling come up?'

'Not really…nothing too strange.' Not unless you count the fact that I've already come up against the name Carstairs, she thought.

He poured her some coffee from the percolator in the office and she sipped the steaming liquid gratefully.

'You must know these people very well—how long have you been in the practice?' she asked.

'About seven years now—it was run by my father originally and I came to take his place when he retired. He died two years ago, but he looked after generations of families in the area and was very much loved.'

'And has your other partner been with you since then?' asked Lisa with interest.

'Terry Newman joined me about five years ago.'

'How sad that your father didn't have much time to enjoy his retirement,' commented Lisa.

Ronan swigged down the rest of his coffee and swilled his cup under the sink. 'He hated retirement—it gave him too much time to do daft things! Eventually he and my mother moved to Glasgow to be nearer my sisters. And now,' he added briskly, 'shall we get off and pay a visit to Mr Fairbairn, one hundred and one years old and still going strong?'

Lisa flicked a quick look at him. Had she touched a raw nerve there? She'd obviously blundered in with a question that had stirred up something in the past that he didn't like—enough to make him change the subject very swiftly indeed.

She said smilingly, as if she hadn't noticed his discomfiture, 'The air up here must be good for you—I've already seen a ninety-year-old today who's been redecorating his house!'

'Gordon Fairbairn lives at Corrie House,' explained Ronan as they drove along through Arrandale. 'It's a good nursing home, but we've been told that it will have to close down soon. It's council run, but they say it's costing too much and they'll move the residents to one in Inverleith—which in my mind would be a disaster. Apart from the fact that most of the residents were born and bred around here and their relatives live near, the stress of a move could kill the frailer ones.'

'That's a terrible shame. Have people put in objections?'

'They certainly have. We're in the middle of trying to raise money to save the place—you could get caffeine poisoning with the amount of coffee mornings the village have held to keep Corrie House going!'

He turned the car into the gateway of a large and gracious-looking house, probably Edwardian, guessed Lisa, with bay windows on either side of an imposing front door, through which could be seen some of the residents seated in the rooms.

'Half the house isn't used,' commented Ronan as they walked up to the door. 'The place does need refurbishing, but the owner leases the house to the council for a peppercorn rent and it's the council's job to pay for repairs.'

'Is the owner a local man?' asked Lisa.

'He's the local bigwig.' Ronan grinned as he rang the bell. 'His name's Sir Richard Carstairs and I come across him from time to time on various committees.'

That name again, thought Lisa wryly. 'Funnily enough, one of the patients this morning works for Sir Richard,' she said. 'Mrs Glendinning is his housekeeper apparently.'

'Ah, yes, she's very proud of her job. It's a huge house and he has a large family so it must be quite hard work.'

A neat little woman wearing a white nurse's cap and a dark

blue uniform appeared at the front door and greeted them, with a specially wide smile for Ronan. Her badge revealed she was the matron, Dilys Conran. He's certainly scored a hit with her, thought Lisa with amusement.

'Good morning, Ronan. I'm so glad you've managed to come and see Mr Fairbairn this morning. I told him you'd be along.'

'Hello, Dilys. Let me introduce you to my new colleague, Dr Lisa Balfour. I'm just showing her a few of our regular patients, because I'm sure she'll be coming over quite a bit.'

Dilys smiled and shook Lisa's hand. 'It's marvellous that someone's come to help Ronan—he's been working so hard on his own. I just hope we'll all still be here for a while. Apparently another blow has fallen on the home—Sir Richard's wanting to put up the rent to the council. That could be the final straw as far as our future is concerned.' She sighed and shook her head. 'We've twenty old folk who love it here and dread being moved.'

Lisa nodded sympathetically. 'That's too bad—it must be so unsettling for everyone, not knowing what the future holds.'

The matron led them through a pleasant sunny room where some of the residents were sitting in a bedroom at the back of the house.

'Mr Fairbairn's chest is bad again,' she explained to the doctors. 'It sounds very congested.'

'He's getting very frail,' said Ronan. 'Only to be expected at his age—he's suffering from heart failure really and all the accompanying problems.'

The elderly man was sitting by the window in a high-backed chair and a rug pulled over his knees.

'Hello, Gordon,' said Ronan in a loud voice, and, going over to him, dropped to his knees so that the patient didn't have to look up at him. 'I've come along with my new partner, Dr Balfour. I wanted to show her around on her first day.'

Twinkling old eyes, now a faded blue, looked up at Lisa and a frail head nodded to her then he looked at Ronan with a quirky little smile and said in a faint voice, 'Got yourself a beautiful colleague, haven't you? That'll make it worth coming to work!'

'Nothing wrong with your eyesight, is there?' remarked Ronan, taking out his stethoscope and bending forward to open the old man's shirt so that he could listen to his chest. 'I hear you're having a bit of chest trouble again…finding it hard to breathe?'

'That I am,' said Mr. Fairbairn faintly.

Ronan listened for a moment then sat back on his heels. 'Would you mind if Dr Balfour had a listen, too—see what she thinks?'

Lisa heard the erratic galloping beat of the old heart and noted the enlarged veins in Mr Fairbairn's neck.

'Rather a rapid pulse,' she murmured.

'What do you expect if a pretty girl comes near me?' the old man growled. Then he looked at them with a rueful smile. 'Not much time left, have I? I know I'm winding down now— but I'm not sorry, I've had a good life and I've no family left.' He put a thin, veined hand on Ronan's arm. 'Now, don't you let any of these medical people try and resuscitate me—I don't want to be hooked up to all those damn wires and tubes. Do you hear me?'

Ronan took the old man's hand. 'No, Gordon,' he said gently. 'We'll follow your wishes, but I'm going to give you some medicine that will make you feel more comfortable—you don't mind that, do you?'

How good Ronan was with his elderly patient, thought Lisa, pleasantly surprised by his gentle compassion and understanding. She glanced across at Dilys, who caught her eye and nodded as if she'd read Lisa's thoughts.

'What do you advise, Dr Gillespie?' asked the matron.

'I think I'll give him some vasodilator drugs—do you agree, Lisa?'

'They'd certainly reduce the workload of his heart. What about blood tests for kidney function and anaemia?'

'Not worth it,' growled the old man. 'Can't you prescribe a slug of whisky? That would do me all the good in the world!'

Ronan chuckled. 'Quite right! I think you should have a wee dram every night—will you see to that, Matron?'

'I'll make a note of it immediately, Doctor…'

They left Mr Fairbairn in his comfy chair, looking out over the beautiful hills.

'His heart's in a bad way,' said Ronan to Dilys as they went back to her office. 'I don't want to stuff him full of drugs, but I think we can make him more comfortable. I'll have a tank of oxygen delivered to help his breathing. I don't want to move the old boy to a hospital. If you can cope, he'd be happier here.'

'It would be cruel to send him to hospital,' agreed Dilys. 'There's nothing they can do there that we can't do.'

'I'll pop in again tomorrow afternoon and see how he's doing on the isosorbide I'm prescribing and if he's having any adverse effects. '

'We'll keep a close eye on him,' Dilys assured him at the door as they left.

'It's very sad that Corrie House may have to close—it's such a lovely place,' remarked Lisa as they walked down the drive.

'Sad indeed,' agreed Ronan. 'I just wish the council would cough up—it's pitiful to think of someone like Gordon Fairbairn being moved at his time of life.'

They discussed the home as they walked down the stone steps that led to where the car was parked.

'If I could do something about the situation, I would,' he sighed.

There had been a cloudburst while they'd been seeing Gordon Fairbairn and a huge puddle had formed at the bottom of the steps.

'These potholes need filling in,' Ronan remarked. 'Like the rest of the place, it's falling into disrepair.' He leapt over the puddle easily, then looked back at Lisa, holding out his hand. 'Come on, I'll help you. Be careful—I don't want another colleague with a broken leg!'

Lisa laughed scornfully. 'I'm OK—I can get over that with no trouble.'

The puddle was wider than Lisa had thought, and the little jump she gave certainly wasn't enough to clear it. With a dull splash she landed in the middle of the water, spattering mud over her skirt and legs. She gave a shriek of disgust and Ronan stepped forward swiftly. He took both her arms and lifted her out and over the puddle.

He looked down at her, a sudden mischievous grin lighting his face. 'I thought you said you could jump over it easily!'

Their eyes locked for a split second in mutual humour, then the smile died on his lips and he took his hands from her arms and stepped away. He was still very close to her, however—close enough for her to see the black lashes fringing his eyes, a slight touch of grey at his temples, the white scar at the corner of his mouth. And suddenly and crazily Lisa wondered what it would be like to put her cheek next to his and feel his lips against hers, to run her finger over that intriguing little scar. Her heart did a tap dance against her ribs, as if she'd just run a few hundred yards down a cobbled street.

Then she took a deep breath. What the hell was she thinking about? He was a colleague, a man she'd only known for a week or two, and in any case Ronan, with the inbuilt confidence that went with the backing of wealth and privilege, was the sort of man she avoided. So easy to be duped by that kind of man—to believe all he said. And the dull ache of the memory of what had happened in Grangeford flooded back to her with horrible clarity.

'You've dirtied that nice suit—there's even a spot of mud on your face,' Ronan remarked lightly, and put up his hand to brush it away from her cheek.

She closed her eyes for a second, trying to suppress that unwelcome feeling of excitement tinged with danger that fluttered through her again. Was she imagining it, or had Ronan felt it, too? She opened her eyes and saw that he was already at the car, bending to inspect a mark on the windscreen, the little incident obviously already completely out of his mind.

Pull yourself together, girl, she told herself robustly as she walked briskly towards the car. She didn't need a man. Her mother had taught her that by example, encouraging Lisa to work hard for everything she had, to rely on no one else and to ensure that she had good qualifications that meant she need never be without a job. Lisa smiled slightly to herself. Her mother had taken such pride in her daughter's achievements, and she would never forget what she'd said on the day Lisa had graduated from medical school, hugging her daughter with tears in her eyes.

'You've made it, my darling—despite all the struggles, you've made it! Now you can always be your own woman—be free to direct your own life!'

CHAPTER THREE

THEY drove for a while in silence and Lisa flicked a quick look at Ronan's serious profile, hoping that he hadn't been aware of the tug of sexual attraction she'd felt for him a few minutes before. When she had arrived in Arrandale she'd believed that after her experience with Trevor Merchant she would be giving men a wide berth for a long time to come. Her mother had been proved right in that instance. He had treated her unpardonably and now she felt appalled and astonished in equal parts that she should be so easily attracted again by a man she'd only been working with for a day!

She leaned back in her seat and tried to concentrate on the spectacular scenery, pushing her extraordinary feelings about Ronan to the back of her mind. She mustn't jeopardise the future by getting involved in any complicated relationships, thank you very much. She was fancy-free, thank heaven, and intended to remain that way for some time!

'Beautiful, isn't it?' Ronan's deep voice broke into her thoughts.

'What? Oh, yes…the scenery. Absolutely! I can't believe how I stuck Grangeford so long! You must love this place.'

'I can't imagine living anywhere else,' he said simply. 'For a long time I haven't been able to do the things I love doing around here—walking, playing golf and fishing. Now you're around, I think I'll be able to relax more.'

'I hope so.'

He was following the main road leading back to the village. 'Now I'm going to take you to a very different place— one that will make you realise that it's not all roses around here. This family are what you might call regular customers of ours.'

He turned a corner into a housing estate that bounded a small industrial area at the other end of the town from the medical centre, and drew up in front of one of the terraced houses. The short path to the front door was littered with paper, old cans and plastic bags, and from the house the sounds of a woman's voice shouting obscenities hit their ears. Lisa met Ronan's eyes with a questioning look and he shrugged eloquently.

'Par for the course, I think,' he said. 'Jean MacCann isn't known for her refinement.'

He rang the doorbell, then knocked loudly. A dog started barking ferociously in the background and a harsh voice shouted at it to shut up. Then a red-faced woman with a tight dirty T-shirt straining over her chest opened the door a crack, looked at them suspiciously and then let them in.

'Kevin's on the couch in the back place,' she said tersely, eyeing Lisa up and down. 'Are you a nurse?'

'This is Dr Balfour, who's just joined the practice—she's coming with me on some visits to get to know the patients.'

Jean McCann grunted in reply, and pushed past them. They followed her to a gloomy room with shabby curtains drawn over the windows and a television blaring in the corner.

Outside a dog was hurling itself at the back door with a ca-
cophony of snarls and barks. In the room the heavy smell of
cigarette smoke and stale beer hung in the air.

A gangling boy of about fourteen sat on the sofa, staring
fixedly at the images on the screen, barely glancing up when
his mother said sharply, 'Doctor's here—let him look at you.'

'He says his throat's sore—had it for days,' she added
loudly, over the noise of the television, and kicked away a
mound of papers and comics by the boy's feet. 'Kevin, open
your mouth and let him see it…'

Ronan squatted by the couch and took out a small torch
from his bag. 'Why didn't he come to the surgery before?' he
asked as he looked down the boy's throat.

Jean looked at him sullenly. 'I haven't got the time, have I?
Besides, I wasn't feeling too good myself—and he won't go on
his own.' The woman took a cigarette from a pack in her skirt
pocket and, having lit it, inhaled deeply. 'What's his throat like?'

Ronan stood up and took out a prescription pad, glancing
irritably at the noise of a gunfight coming from the screen in
the corner.

'Not very good—his tonsils are enlarged and rather infected. I'll give him some antibiotics. Are you allergic to pen-
icillin?' he said to the boy, then paused for a moment and
looked towards the blaring television. 'Do you think you
could turn that thing off, please, for a few minutes?'

For the first time Kevin showed signs of animation as the
screen was silenced. 'Wha'd'ya do that for?' he demanded aggressively. 'I was watching that.' He made to get up to put it
back on.

Ronan put a hand on the boy's shoulder. 'Wait a minute,
Kevin, I want to feel the glands in your neck first.'

He ran his fingers lightly down the sides of the boy's neck. 'They're pretty enlarged—you must finish the course of medicine I give you and drink plenty of liquids. Come and see me next week if things haven't improved.'

Kevin nodded morosely and turned the television back on, very loudly. Ronan's and Lisa's eyes met in mutual exasperation.

'Right, then, we'll go now, Mrs McCann. Plenty of other patients to see.'

The woman let them out of the house and Lisa took a deep breath of fresh air as they walked back to the main street where Ronan had parked the car.

'Pretty smoky in there,' she murmured.

'Too many of my patients smoke—that woman has bronchitis every winter but I doubt she'll ever take my advice.' He looked at her with a droll smile. 'So now you've had a sample of the patients in Annandale—pretty much the same complaints as the people you've left behind in Grangeford, I suspect?'

She laughed. 'Absolutely! There are a lot of Mrs MacCanns in Grangeford.'

The wind whipped Lisa's hair into a golden halo around her head and her hazel eyes sparkled with humour. Ronan stared at her for a second then opened the car door quickly. Every now and then Lisa startled him by looking so damned attractive. Unwillingly his mind clicked back to the sudden and unexpected treacherous tingle of excitement that had flickered through him when he'd helped her over the puddle at the nursing home. He reflected with a kind of horrified astonishment that it wouldn't have taken much to make him put his arms around her waist and hold her very close to him, her soft body pressing against his.

Irritably he eased himself into the car seat and pushed the key into the ignition. The trouble was, he was sex starved. After Maisie he had vowed it would be a long time before he looked at another woman again—he'd had his fingers burned once and that was enough. And now, he thought gloomily, it was going to be impossible to concentrate on work if he felt this thumping physical attraction for Lisa every time she came near him!

He reversed the car quickly out of the parking space and said briskly, 'Time to go back to the surgery and grab some lunch. I've got a lot of paperwork to do and a meeting this evening, but there's a well-baby clinic this afternoon and I'd be grateful if you'd take that.'

Lisa looked at him curiously, aware of his change of mood. 'Of course,' she replied lightly. 'I love doing baby clinics.'

He drove up the main street and back to The Coppice Medical Centre, then peered more closely through the windscreen as they approached.

'Hello,' he murmured. 'What the hell's happening here?'

A small knot of people had gathered near the entrance and were gazing down at a figure lying on the ground.

'Looks like someone's had an accident,' said Lisa.

Ronan drew the car up to the kerb. They leapt out, shouldered their way through the gaping onlookers and knelt down beside the victim. It was Cora Simmonds lying stretched out on the pavement, with a very pale face, her eyes fluttering open and shut.

'Not again!' groaned Ronan.

Lisa looked at him questioningly. 'This happens regularly?'

'Spontaneous hypoglycaemia,' he said succinctly. 'She's diabetic —she's always going on a damn crash diet and probably hasn't eaten anything for hours. Luckily Val hasn't been affected with diabetes, although they're twins.'

'So, coupled with the insulin she probably took earlier, that's tipped her into a hypoglycaemic attack,' remarked Lisa.

'Precisely! She's been told again and again to be careful.'

'Val's ringing for an ambulance,' volunteered a young woman, who had been holding Cora's hand. 'Cora just staggered out of the door mumbling something a few minutes ago, then she collapsed. She seems so clammy and pale…'

'The ambulance has a long way to come—it could be ages,' said Ronan. 'There's a glucometer in my bag in the back of the car, Lisa. I'll take a reading of her blood sugar.'

The crowd watched silently as Lisa handed him the small instrument and he took a pinprick of blood from Cora's finger. 'As I suspected,' he said grimly, looking at the reading. 'It's under one…'

'Intravenous glucose, then?' asked Lisa.

'Yes,' Ronan said tersely.

She passed Ronan a pre-dosed phial of glucose from the bag and watched as he injected it into Cora's arm.

'That should do the trick.' Ronan knelt back on his heels and took Cora's pulse, pressing two fingers against her wrist over the radial artery. After a few seconds he nodded. 'That's better—hopefully this should bring her round soon.'

As if on cue, Cora began to stir, looking around her with a bewildered air. 'What am I doing here?' she asked faintly.

'You passed out—forgot to have your sugar, didn't you?'

Val came running out of the surgery looking very distressed. 'Is she all right?' she asked tearfully. 'I suddenly noticed she was behaving oddly—not herself at all—and then she wandered outside…'

'She'll be fine, Val. I take it the ambulance is coming? I'd like her to go to hospital and get into balance again.' Ronan stood up and turned to the curious bystanders. 'Now, haven't you all got homes to go to?' he asked, not unkindly. 'Cora will be OK, I assure you.'

'Are you sure, Ronan?' Val dabbed at her eyes. 'I do try and keep and eye on her, but she takes no notice of what I say…'

'Perhaps they'll read her the Riot Act at the hospital—has she been on yet another diet?'

Val nodded. 'I probably shouldn't tease her about her weight. It's my fault—she's been on a "one good meal a day" regime. I knew it was silly.'

'Absolutely stupid for a diabetic,' agreed Ronan.

'If she really wants to lose weight, why don't you help her follow a sensible diet for a while?' suggested Lisa, putting a rug she'd found in Ronan's car over Cora. 'Really supporting her could make all the difference.'

'That's a good idea, and maybe I could diet with her. I certainly need to lose weight as much as my sister,' sighed Val.

The ambulance arrived and two paramedics jumped out and were quickly informed by Ronan about Cora's condition.

'You go with her, Val,' he said. 'We can manage here without you for a while…no problem.'

Val looked uncertainly at each of the doctors. 'Are you sure?'

'Of course we are,' said Lisa. 'I can answer a telephone as easily as anyone, I dare say!'

'But…but you don't know the patients…'

'Then I'll learn quickly.' Lisa laughed. 'Now, get in the ambulance and stop fussing!'

'Looks as if your first day in work is going to be a baptism of fire,' remarked Ronan drily as they went into the building.

'I can cope. What time does the baby clinic start?'

'In about an hour's time. Rachel Burns, the practice nurse, will be coming in to help. She works on a part-time basis. Can you man the phone until then?'

'Of course,' said Lisa airily. On cue, the phone started ringing and she picked it up. 'Coppice Medical Centre,' she said. 'How can I help you?'

'Dilys Conran, Matron of Corrie House Nursing Home here. I think I recognize your voice—is it Dr Balfour? We met earlier today?'

'Yes, it is. What can I do?'

'Could Ronan come over as soon as possible? Since you left, Gordon Fairbairn's condition has deteriorated. I think his heart is in complete failure and he probably hasn't long to go. He's asking for the doctor—he's always been fond of Ronan.'

'He's here right now. Dilys Conran,' she explained, handing the phone over to Ronan.

He listened for a second. 'I'm on my way,' he said. 'Tell Gordon I'll be with him soon.' He put down the phone and turned to Lisa. 'Keep everything ticking over. I must go and say goodbye to the old man—I've known him a long time, and he was a great friend of my father's.'

Lisa nodded understandingly. 'That's one of the hard parts of the job, isn't it? Losing a patient you've looked after for many years. Don't worry, I'll be fine.'

Ronan hesitated for a second before he went and he smiled rather sadly at her. 'I can't help having my favourites—and although it was obvious Gordon wasn't going to last much longer, I shall miss him.'

Lisa watched him striding out to the car and reflected how different a character Ronan was to Trevor Merchant, the head partner in her previous practice. As a doctor Trevor had maintained an unemotional distance from his patients, completely lacking in warmth, and while Lisa could understand that it was often better not to get too involved in patients' problems, sometimes she'd wondered if he liked any of them at all! Her first impression of Ronan had been that he was an aloof man—now she was beginning to realise that he had an affection for those in his care that was very engaging.

She heard Ronan's car accelerating down the road as he sped off towards the nursing home. She looked around her rather nervously. Her first day in the practice and she was in charge of the place. She just hoped nothing too terrible would happen in the next few hours!

In fact, the afternoon passed very pleasantly, with about fifteen babies to be seen—some for routine vaccinations, some for weight checks and others whose mothers had concerns about them. Rachel Burns was a very curvy woman with an infectious laugh and a comforting and reassuring manner with the new young mothers, and she and Lisa took to one another at once. At the end of the session Rachel made them both a cup of tea and produced a large home-made cake.

'You will have a piece, won't you?' she appealed to Lisa. 'It won't make me feel so guilty about having some! Usually Cora and Val would help me out. Now, I suppose, from what you told me about Cora's hypo attack, they won't be having any for some time.'

'She'll have to be much more careful to eat a balanced diet at the right time,' agreed Lisa. 'But go on—give me a small slice!'

'And then I'll have to go and collect the children from school and have the usual battle with them to do their homework,' sighed Rachel, finishing her piece of cake in two mouthfuls and cutting herself another small sliver. 'It's like starting another day's work when I get home. Wait till you have children. They take over your life—especially,' she added gloomily, 'when you have a husband like mine who's on shift work.'

Lisa grinned. 'Go on—I'm sure you love it really. But having children isn't in my game plan at the moment— that's a long way off.'

Rachel looked at Lisa shrewdly as she pulled on her coat and picked up a large shopping basket. 'Oh, really? Can't think why you've not been snapped up before—you must have had hundreds of men after you.'

'Not the right ones, Rachel, I'm afraid,' replied Lisa briskly. 'Anyway, I think I can do without a man to complicate my life at the moment. I want to concentrate on finding a place to live and exploring the beautiful countryside round Arrandale.'

'You never know what's round the corner. I bet there are loads of men searching for a gorgeous girl like you. For goodness' sake, there's one under your very nose! Ronan Gillespie's been on his own for far too long!'

'Romance and work aren't a good combination,' observed Lisa lightly, draining her cup and rinsing it under the tap. 'And I don't think I'm his type and I'm certainly not ready to settle down yet.'

Rachel laughed. 'I can't think of a better type than you— I'd have said you were very well matched. But make the most of your freedom, I say! In the meantime, I'm really glad you've joined the practice—poor old Ronan's been working his socks off.'

She went to the door and turned back with a parting shot. 'But I'm going to keep my eyes skinned for a suitable bachelor all the same. See you tomorrow!'

She plodded off and Lisa grinned. Having a ring on her finger was not something she wanted for a very long time—she didn't need a man in order to enjoy life. She glanced at her watch. It was half past three and she started to update the notes on the baby patients while she was in the office. She began to immerse herself in paperwork, jumping slightly when someone tapped on the glass. She looked up. A startlingly attractive woman was standing in Reception. She had silky dark brown hair dropping in a straight bob round her face and was smartly dressed in a tan trouser suit.

Lisa went to the counter. 'Can I help you?'

The woman looked slightly surprised. 'Have the Simmonds twins left?' she asked. She had a low husky voice and unusual pale green eyes fringed by long eyelashes.

Lisa laughed. 'Not at all—I'm just filling in for a short time as Cora's not well. I'm actually Dr Gillespie's new partner.'

The woman looked surprised. 'Indeed? I didn't know he was taking anyone else on.' She smiled charmingly at Lisa, her glance sweeping appraisingly over her. 'You don't come from around here, do you?'

'No. I'm from the North of England—Grangeford.'

'I see… Well, I hope you take to the rural life up here after the bustle of life there. It's very beautiful in Arrandale, of course, but there can be drawbacks to living in the country.' She gave a little laugh and held out a slim hand. 'Perhaps I could introduce myself. My name is Maisie Cowper and I'm just paying a social visit to see Dr Gillespie. He's an old friend, and as I'm back in the area now and was just passing the practice, I thought I'd look in. I know he'd want to know I'm around again.'

Maisie's smile was dazzling, revealing even white teeth and appealing little dimples at the sides of her mouth. An engaging manner, reflected Lisa, returning her smile.

'I'm pleased to meet you. I'm Lisa Balfour. I'm afraid I'm not sure when Ronan will be back—he's visiting a patient.'

'Ah, healing the sick. Ronan always was very dedicated…' said Maisie lightly, a little chuckle in her voice.

'I'll tell him you've been. Perhaps he could give you a call…have you a mobile number?'

Maisie looked at a gold watch encasing her slim wrist. 'Damn! I've got to go and view some properties so I can't wait, but tell him I'll pop in again soon, will you? I won't bother leaving my number.'

She gave a brilliant smile and walked out, looking chic and smart and not, thought Lisa with amusement, like any of the usual Arrandale villagers. Then her thoughts were interrupted by the phone, and Ronan's voice at the other end.

'Hello, Lisa—just reporting back. I'll be with you soon. Gordon passed away peacefully and I've done all the formalities. Have you been OK?'

'Yes, fine. I'll give you the messages when you get back.'

She replaced the receiver, briefly still intrigued by the vibrant Maisie Cowper and wondering where Maisie featured in Ronan's life. Were they old friends and nothing more, or was Maisie hoping to become closer? Lisa shrugged her shoulders crossly. It wasn't any of her business who Ronan's friends were, and just because a beautiful woman came in and made enquiries about him, it didn't mean that they were an item. She stared at her reflection in the small mirror by the handbasin and shook her head shamefacedly, recognising in herself a tiny seed of jealousy, and all because she'd felt a bolt of sexual attraction towards Ronan that morning. And how sad was that, Lisa thought angrily to herself. Becoming paranoid about a pleasant woman who'd visited Ronan because they were old friends.

She made a note of all the messages and calls and stuck them on the computer screen in the office, then got back to her paperwork. She had to put that man out of her head, move out of his house and get on with her life!

Ronan returned about half an hour later and put down a small package on the desk. 'Gordon knew he was going,' he told Lisa, 'and he insisted I take his medals from the war.'

He undid the paper around the little parcel and spread the contents on the table. Beside the medals was a sepia photograph of a young man in military uniform with his arm around a pretty girl.

'That's Gordon with his wife, Hetty,' he said softly. 'She died a few years ago now, but she was always a lovely-looking woman. He never got over losing her.'

Lisa looked at the faded photo. 'They look a very handsome couple and very much in love. Did they have any children?'

'Sadly, no, but they seemed so content in each other's company that it didn't seem to matter.'

Lisa sighed. 'Then they were lucky in that.'

'Now—any messages? Have you heard how Cora is?'

'Yes. Val rang to say she was stable, but they're keeping her in overnight for observation. Oh, and a Maisie Cowper came to see you. She said it was a social call and she'd call back later. She's back in this area apparently.'

Ronan looked up at her quickly, as if startled. 'What? Who

did you say?' His voice was loud, almost a shout. 'Maisie Cowper? She came here to the surgery?'

'Yes,' said Lisa, surprised at his reaction. 'She said she was passing by and that she was an old friend of yours.'

'Did she indeed? Did you tell her when I'd be back?'

'I told her you were visiting a patient…'

'So she knows I'll be back this afternoon, I suppose?'

'Sorry…' Lisa's voice faltered, looking at his expression. 'Did I do the wrong thing?'

His face relaxed slightly and he gave a wry smile. 'Not your fault. It's just, well, she's the last person…'

Then his voice trailed away and his face froze for a second. He looked past Lisa into the reception area as the door opened and Maisie entered the room.

'For heaven's sake,' he muttered. 'Not Maisie. Not again…'

His expression darkened. Lisa looked at him with puzzlement—what on earth was wrong?

'Are you OK, Ronan?'

He didn't answer, just stared at Maisie. Then he turned back to Lisa urgently.

'Look,' he muttered, 'I've got to do something. Forgive me, but I'm going to have to kiss you!'

Lisa looked at him in astonishment. 'You're going to have to *what*?'

'Do this…'

He pulled her roughly towards him and put his arms around her, pressing her body to his hard frame, then before she could draw breath his mouth was on hers, firm and unyielding. She could feel his heart thudding against her body as they stood, locked together in an embrace that seemed to last for ever.

Lisa's thoughts spun round in her head—what the hell was happening and just what did Ronan think he was doing? An extraordinary mixture of fury, indignation and—even more crazily—enjoyment whirled through her. She should be pushing him away, slapping his face, anything to stop him in his tracks. Instead, she felt herself responding to him, pressing herself as urgently to him as he was to her.

A short laugh came from behind them, and a dry voice said, 'Oho! So this is how the lands lies, Ronan—you are a dark horse!'

Lisa twisted out of Ronan's arms and looked round, acutely embarrassed. Whatever would the woman think? She and Ronan were meant to be at work, for heaven's sake!

Ronan turned to the visitor. 'Ah…Maisie, this is a surprise,' he said, his voice over-smooth. 'Lisa told me you'd called in before and that you were in the area. This is Lisa's first day in the practice…'

A peculiar expression passed over Maisie's flushed face—was it anguish or anger? 'And you're showing her the ropes, eh?' she said softly, a stiff little smile on her lips. 'Don't worry, Ronan, you've made it plain exactly what your partnership is, and now I know what's going on, I'll be off. No point in staying where I'm not wanted.'

'Lisa and I—' began Ronan.

'Don't bother to explain,' said Maisie curtly. 'It's perfectly obvious. Stephen and I are having a trial separation and I thought perhaps you and I could rekindle what we once had together. I'm glad I know what's happening.'

She drew herself up proudly and then turned on her heel and marched out, slamming the door of the surgery hard behind her.

There was silence for a second. Lisa touched her burning lips and stared at Ronan in bewilderment, then indignation took over and she said angrily, 'Maisie may know what's going on, Ronan Gillespie, but I don't. What the hell came over you just now?'

CHAPTER FOUR

RONAN looked at Lisa ruefully, hands held up in apology. 'What can I say? I was desperate…'

'Thank you very much.'

'I mean I had to do something drastic to bring it home to Maisie that I wasn't available. I guessed she'd come back to try and start our relationship up again, and it was all I could think of…a dramatic action that would stop her thinking she could come back into my life.'

'So you used me to demonstrate that? I don't like being used, Ronan.' Lisa's hazel eyes sparked across at him. 'The next time someone from your past comes in, perhaps you could just tell them you don't want to go out with them, rather than grabbing the nearest female.'

Ronan's eyes swept over her furious face. He sighed and grimaced. 'You're right—it was a stupid thing to do. I don't know what came over me. All I can say is that Maisie doesn't care who she hurts…'

'She seemed very pleasant to me. To be honest, I think it's a cruel way to show you weren't interested in her. She obviously thought you still felt something for her.'

His mouth tightened and he frowned. 'You don't know

her. When she wants something or someone, nothing can stop her—I know, I was once engaged to her. Believe me, she can be very cruel.'

So Maisie was the ex-fiancée! Lisa recalled the odd remarks that she'd heard, inferring that the break-up had caused his unhappiness. She nodded coolly. 'I see.'

'You heard her say she wanted to rekindle our relationship. Well, Maisie doesn't take no for an answer and I wanted to demonstrate unequivocally that she means nothing to me. I don't even want to see her socially.'

Maisie had certainly got under Ronan's skin, Lisa mused. She flicked a glance at his good-looking but rather patrician face—he was just the type of man who would do what he wanted to achieve his own ends, she decided. He'd been brought up in that comfortable social stratum of wealth and privilege to believe that he was always right—never mind how hurtful his actions could be. It was a scenario she was only too familiar with. She regarded Ronan stonily.

'I can't believe you couldn't have told her the simple truth—and if you think that the only way to show her you no longer want her is a good reason for grabbing me, you must be mad.'

His expression darkened. 'You don't know the whole story, Lisa. She and I have a very bad history…but I don't want to go into that.' Then he shook his head and put his hands lightly on her shoulders, holding her gaze with his own. 'Whatever made me do it, it was a crass thing to do, and I took a liberty. Will you forgive me?'

What an amazing blue his eyes were, thought Lisa, like the Mediterranean. And there were little green flecks in them. His expression was penitent but persuasive, and his mouth had a wan smile. And then he added softly, 'But it was a wonderful experience nevertheless…'

Lisa forgot the amazing eyes for a moment, jolted back into annoyance and stepped away from him. 'A wonderful experience? What the hell are you talking about? It was a diabolical liberty and I ought to walk straight out of this job…'

But even as she spat the words out, Lisa thought guiltily that it was true. What he had done had felt so wonderful, so…so dangerously right, and at another time, in another place, who knew what it would have led to? A little voice inside her whispered that she would love to do it again, and wasn't there a tiny jolt of relief that he didn't want Maisie after all? It was all so damned confusing, she thought crossly. She seemed to have learned nothing from her past experience. She irritably brushed a tendril of hair from her forehead and looked at him angrily.

Ronan put his hand up as if to stop her from interrupting. 'You have every reason to walk out but, please, don't do that. What I did was unpardonable. All I can say is that it was done in the heat of the moment—I wasn't trying to make fun of you or take advantage. Can't you forgive me?'

Lisa felt herself starting to weaken—those periwinkle blue eyes looked so honestly into hers, nearly persuading her that he'd had no choice but to kiss her! She pushed the thought away and scowled at him.

'You grab me without warning, hold me in a clinch for minutes on end in front of an ex-girlfriend on my first day at work, and expect me to forgive you?'

Again his eyes held hers, this time warily, like a naughty boy who wasn't sure how severe his punishment was going to be, and although Lisa still didn't know just exactly what had caused the split between Ronan and Maisie, she was prepared to believe that it had to have been something pretty earth-shattering. Suddenly from nowhere a bubble of amusement welled up inside her and she had to choke back a gurgle of laughter, tickled by the sheer cheek of his action.

'I am not, Ronan Gillespie, candy in a shop to be sampled whenever you feel like it, and it certainly wasn't part of the job description—but, yes, you're forgiven. This time!'

His sudden smile lit up his expression, the angular planes of his face softening. 'You're a sport. I certainly shouldn't have used you as a decoy. Now, please, let me take you out to dinner to make up for my appalling manners.'

Lisa shook her head. 'I don't think so, Ronan. I'm pretty tired. I'm going straight back to the house to have a bath and an early night. I think we've seen enough of each other today!'

'Then I'll take you out another time—but make sure you have some supper. I'm sure Betty will have left something in the fridge.'

'I'll have a sandwich in my room,' she said firmly. 'See you tomorrow.' She paused for a second as she walked towards the door and looked back at him. 'I think it would be better if we forgot all about this incident—pretend it never happened. Don't you?'

She marched out of the surgery, letting the door bang behind her, and Ronan watched her departure with a little smile. Forget the incident? Who was she kidding? Lisa may have acted outraged when he had kissed her, but he hadn't been deceived. She had enjoyed it as much as he had, her body responding to his like an electric charge through a light bulb. He shouldn't have done it—but it had been marvelous, and part of that excitement had been because he'd realised as he'd kissed her that Lisa had loved it, too! He had almost forgotten what it felt like to have a beautiful woman's body pressed to his, to feel a soft mouth against his lips. So much for good resolutions, he reflected wryly.

He supposed he ought to concentrate on the results of the patients' blood tests that had come through that day. He frowned as he sat down at the computer to read his e-mails, but instead of seeing them he could only picture Lisa's face in front of him as he'd taken her in his arms, the shock in her eyes as he'd kissed her. Seeing Maisie again out of the blue had shaken him so much that he had jeopardised a working relationship by a stupidly impulsive act, hoping to hammer home to Maisie that he was not available.

And now that he knew what it was like to kiss Lisa, how was he going to stop thinking about her—and avoiding her when they were together at the house? Because there was one thing he was certain of—he was not going to get involved with a woman again for a very, very long time.

Lisa pressed her hot forehead against the cool window-pane and watched Ronan's dog in the garden below, chasing rabbits with joyful barks. She felt a jumble of emotions—resentment that Ronan's kiss had made for awkwardness between them before they'd barely started working together and guilty excitement at the memory of his touch. She closed her eyes for a second, reliving the firmness of his mouth on hers, the slight roughness of his chin and the comforting muscular hardness of his body. But, of course, she told herself harshly, Ronan had only kissed her to send a message to Maisie that he wasn't available—not because he'd really wanted to. She had to forget about that kiss and the reasons Ronan might have for hating Maisie so much—put it out of her mind.

Impatiently she turned away from the window and got into bed, trying to calm her mind as she watched the light dying outside and the dark clouds scudding across the night sky. She didn't need Ronan anyway. How often had her mother told her to keep her independence as long as she could? Her mother had been a wonderful example of resilience and fortitude while bringing up a child alone. She had learned about betrayal the hard way and had begged Lisa never to rely on a man too much.

Lisa hugged her knees to her chest and felt for a moment a terrible longing to see her mother again, to hear her wise advice. Her death had made Lisa ricochet towards the first man that showed an interest in her, and Trevor Merchant had been a terrible mistake. She mustn't have another disaster with Ronan, however much she was attracted to him.

She clicked the light off by her bed and lay down. The sooner she was out of Ronan's house, the easier it would be to put distance between them. She heard the door bang downstairs as he came home, his footsteps on the stairs as he went up to his room, and she shivered slightly, pulling the covers around her as she tried to get to sleep. When she did finally drift off, it was Ronan's face that featured in her dreams.

It was almost a relief that the next few days were incredibly busy and any conversation between Ronan and Lisa could be restricted to work matters. When they were together at the house they maintained an awkward sort of politeness, and the incident that had happened in the surgery was never mentioned, although it seemed to act as an invisible barrier between them.

One day they had a meeting after work with Val and Cora. Ronan was courteous and brisk as they discussed patients' missed appointments, the drug budget and a new computer system for the surgery, but there was no small talk with Lisa. When they'd finished, Val suggested that they go into the village for an Italian meal at a new little restaurant. Ronan caught Lisa's eye briefly, then gathered up his papers.

'Some other time,' he said lightly. 'I've got a game of squash lined up.'

Lisa sighed inwardly. This awkwardness between them didn't make work easier. A pleasant meal might have eased the situation.

By the time Friday came, Lisa felt as if she'd been working for years at the practice. She was ready for the weekend and to move her things out of Ronan's house and into Bill Garrity's cottage. She brought up the next patient's notes on the screen—a young man called Jo Cutler. He was the last patient of the day and had been referred to his GP, having attended the A and E department at Inverleith hospital the day before. Jo was a large, strapping young man with a healthy-looking countenance who looked as if he'd never had a day's illness in his life.

'It's my breathing, Doctor,' he explained. 'I was playing football after work at the local club, but I began to get so breathless and dizzy when I ran about the pitch I had to sit down on the sidelines. I can't understand it—never had it happen to me before, but this last week I've had a few of these little spells of dizziness.'

'You certainly look fit,' said Lisa. 'What's your job?'

'I'm a postman—cycle all over the village, up and down hills.'

'Then you get plenty of exercise. Stand up and let me sound out your chest. Have you had any pain with this shortage of breath over the last few days?'

'Sort of fleeting pains—nothing dramatic, and if I hadn't been out of breath and forced to sit down I probably wouldn't have noticed them. Last night I got a bit worried and went to Inverleith A and E. I felt rather foolish, especially as they couldn't find anything after a chest X-ray and ECG. I thought it might have been asthma.'

'I'd say you've been very wise to have it checked out—there's got to be some reason it's happening.' said Lisa, tucking her stethoscope back in her pocket when she'd listened to his chest. 'You say this happened while you were running round the pitch? Do you feel OK when you're sitting still?'

'Absolutely fine. The doctor in A and E suggested it might be stress-related, but I don't feel under stress. I really enjoy my job—wouldn't want anything to jeopardise it.'

Lisa nodded. 'I'm not so sure about the stress-related diagnosis—especially as this seems to be induced by exercise.' She smiled at him. 'I think I'll ask you to do a short test for me. I want you to run up and down the surgery stairs three or four times—see how you react after that.'

Dutifully, Jo went into the corridor and to the interest of waiting patients pounded up and down the short flight of stairs until Lisa told him to come into her room again.

She clipped a peg onto his finger and watched the monitor to which it was wired. 'This tells me what your sats are—that is, the oxygent saturation level in your blood,' she explained. She frowned slightly as the results flickered on the little screen. 'I wonder if you'd mind Dr Gillespie looking at you and giving his opinion?'

Jo shrugged. 'Sure. Two heads are better than one, I suppose.'

Lisa pressed a button to call Ronan in his surgery. 'Sorry to interrupt you, Ronan, but I'd appreciate a second opinion here when you've a moment.'

'Be with you in a minute,' he replied.

Lisa felt an annoying little ripple of apprehension before Ronan came into the room. This was work and she was a professional, so she had to ignore the tension between the two of them and push the incident of that kiss firmly to the back of her mind. Nevertheless, when Ronan appeared her stomach did a double somersault—he was so damned attractive, his presence and personality seeming to fill the room.

'You know Jo Cutler, of course?'

Ronan smiled at Jo. 'Some time since I've seen you, Jo. What's the problem?'

'Jo's had breathlessness and dizzy bouts when playing football. A and E did X-rays and an ECG but nothing came to light. Asthma has been ruled out. However, the sats on his oxygen level are lower than they should be for a fit young man of his age. One thing occurs to me and I wondered if you agreed…'

Ronan nodded. 'Go ahead.'

'Pulmonary emboli?'

'I think that's a probable explanation for the inexplicable breathlessness,' agreed Ronan.

Jo looked alarmed. 'What does that mean then?'

'Well, you'll need to have a special lung scan to confirm this, but it could be—and I emphasise could be—that you have a shower of tiny blood clots silting up the vessels in your lungs.'

'Hell!' muttered the young man.

'Don't worry,' Lisa said quickly, looking at the expression on the young man's face. 'There are very effective drugs we can give you that dissolve clots and also prevent them from forming, but we need to make sure that this is the cause of your symptoms.'

'I thought you only got that sort of thing when you were old,' said Jo.

'It's true that you are young for this to happen—but you'd be surprised how often it occurs in your age group. You're very fit otherwise, and once we've made a final diagnosis from the scan I'm sure you'll be back playing football again.'

'Is it serious?'

'Anything that hinders the blood getting to the heart or lungs is serious,' said Ronan gently. 'For that reason we want you to go into hospital straight away.'

'What? Right now?' Jo looked shocked and dumb-founded—a look that Ronan and Lisa had seen many times on patients who had just received unexpected and disturbing news about their health.

'I'll ring the RMO—the resident medical officer,' said Lisa, 'and he'll prioritise a scan for you, but will probably give you injections of heparin straight away.'

'What's that for?' asked the bewildered young man.

'That will thin the blood and disperse any clots. If our diagnosis is correct you'll then probably have oral warfarin. Look,' added Lisa reassuringly, 'this is perfectly treatable. It may be a familial thing since you've no injury like a fracture which can produce clotting when, say, the leg is immobilised.'

'I seem to recall that several years ago your mother had a DVT in her leg after a long plane flight,' said Ronan. 'She was in a lot of pain and her leg was swollen when she came to see me.'

Jo looked startled. 'That's a deep vein thrombosis, right? That's interesting, because last week I flew back from the Canaries with my girlfriend—but it wasn't all that long a flight, and it was a few days ago. My legs weren't painful but they were very stiff.'

'It doesn't have to be a very long flight for this to happen,' explained Lisa. 'You're a very tall man and I expect you didn't have much leg room to allow for movement.'

Jo grinned. 'You can say that again—we were packed in like sardines.'

'Is there anyone who can drive you to the hospital? I'll inform them you're on your way.'

'My girlfriend's in the waiting room—she'll take me.'

'Then off you go. And don't worry, you did entirely the right thing to come in immediately.'

Ronan's voice was upbeat and positive and the young man looked less worried. 'So you think I'll be all right?'

'We're not minimising anything—but you've been wise enough to get advice when you first had these symptoms. I'm sure you'll be fine.'

When Jo had left the room, Ronan remained, sitting on the edge of the desk. He looked at Lisa with a nod of approval.

'A pretty shrewd diagnosis Lisa,' he remarked. 'I'm sure there are other instances of DVT in Jo's family if I looked back in the notes.' He laughed. 'You wouldn't think, looking at Jo, that he had a thing wrong with him.'

'That's why I was suspicious when there seemed to be a discrepancy between what he looked like and the seriousness of his symptoms, although his ECG and X-ray were completely normal.' She gave him a faint smile and said almost reluctantly, 'It…it was good to have someone else's input.'

His eyes danced back at her. 'Despite what you think of me?' he said drily.

Lisa's smile widened, although she replied rather primly, 'I respect your opinion, as a professional.'

'Ah, I see.'

Their eyes locked for a long second, and suddenly there was a lightening of the tension between them. Funny, Lisa thought, how discussion of a patient could bring two people together!

Ronan stepped nearer to her, and said quietly, 'I think we need to talk Lisa...don't you?'

She bit her lip, looking at him warily. She didn't want to get serious with him again. 'What is there to say? We agreed to put that...that incident behind us.'

He put his hands on her shoulders, and his touch sent a shiver of excitement through her body, his deep blue eyes looking into hers. 'But we haven't put it behind us, have we, Lisa? It's still there, stopping us from acting normally with each other, creating a pretty brittle atmosphere.' His hands tightened slightly. 'For heaven's sake, please, let me take you out tonight for dinner—just for a chat and to give you my explanation for my behaviour. I still feel guilty about it. You're moving out tomorrow, and it would be a good idea to sort things out before then. What do you think?'

Lisa's mind raced. Just how sensible would it be to go out for the evening with a man who made her adrenalin pump like super-octane fuel around her body despite her vow not to get involved with him. And yet she had to work with Ronan, and she didn't want the atmosphere between them to get worse—she'd learned from her last job how ghastly life could be if communications broke down between colleagues.

'OK,' she said at last. 'If you really think so.'

That sudden brilliant smile illuminated Ronan's face, the small white scar crinkling against his mouth. 'Then we'll go to the Potarch Inn,' he said. 'It's one of my favourite places in the hills above Arrandale on the river Riach—I'd like to show it to you.'

She couldn't deny that she really wanted to know more about Ronan Gillespie and his past, find out why he had become entangled with Maisie Cowper and why he hated her so much now. She tried to ignore the little voice that whispered in her head, that whatever her reservations, just the thought of being alone with Ronan made her feel something like exhilaration!

The little fishing inn Ronan had chosen to take her was beyond the village in the hills, and by its garden the broad river Riach wended its way down to Arrandale. At that point there were willow trees bending their branches into the water, and the water glinted and sparkled in the sun as it rushed, foaming, over the boulders.

Lisa should have felt relaxed in this beautiful setting, but she felt as tense as a violin string—just why on earth had she agreed to come? Being alone with Ronan was dangerous, she thought wryly, bad for her blood pressure and her peace of mind. The simple fact was that she was having a meal alone with a man she fancied like mad, and it had been a long time since that had happened. But, of course, it wasn't a date as such, was it? Just a friendly evening with a colleague, getting to know each other better for work's sake.

She sat back in her chair, watching Ronan's tall rangy figure as he wended his way through the tables with their drinks.

He was wearing jeans and an open-necked white shirt, and he looked cool and sexy, every woman's eye on him as he passed by. One or two of them were obviously patients. She could hear them murmuring, 'Good evening Dr Gillespie,' and gazing after him curiously to see who he was with.

He handed her a glass of cool white wine and smiled down at her as he eased himself into the chair by her side. She was acutely aware of his maleness, his physicality, even the golden hairs on the backs of his hands.

'You look great,' he said. 'You never bought that outfit in Arrandale, I'll bet.'

He swept an admiring glance over the ice-blue silk trouser suit she was wearing, the colour complementing her tanned neck and arms and the honey hair that brushed her shoulders.

She laughed. 'A lucky buy from a boutique in Grangeford. It does at least have quite good shops, if nothing else.'

'We'll sit out here while we have a drink, but it's going to get quite cool soon—besides being bitten by midges—so I think we'll go in for our food.'

'And what do you recommend from the menu?' asked Lisa, taking a long sip of wine and hoping that on an empty stomach it would stop the butterflies fluttering inside her.

'The steak and ale pie is great here, but if you fancy anything else…'

'That'll be fine.' She looked around at the magnificent scenery and turned to him politely. 'It's absolutely beautiful here—is the building very old?'

'The inn's two hundred years old. It used to be a coaching stop, and now fishermen come here for the salmon in the Riach.'

Lisa twirled her glass in her hand and wondered what other

small talk she could make, then suddenly made up her mind to address the subject that really interested her. After all, wasn't that one of the reasons they'd come here anyway?

'So tell me about Maisie,' she said baldly. 'You loved her once. Why do you hate her now—what really caused the break-up between you?'

Ronan raised his eyebrows slightly at her directness, smiling slightly, and leant forward in his seat, his elbows on his knees, and gazed across the garden to the river beyond.

'It's not as simple as that. For a start, I was never in love with Maisie. I was introduced to her when she lent my father some money. She had a good reputation when it came to figures, investments, things like that, but I think it rested more on personality than ability.'

'What did your father want to invest in?'

Ronan sighed. 'When he retired he had time on his hands and decided he'd like to put up an alternative health centre in Arrandale in a smart new building. My father was always a great one for sudden enthusiasms and very persuasive, and Maisie agreed to lend him the money. But the health centre didn't take off.'

'And she wanted her money back, I guess?'

'Of course. And naturally with interest, as had been agreed. However, she suggested we have a meal together to discuss the project and what we could do to save the business, which seemed perfectly reasonable.'

'And then the affair started?'

Ronan swirled the wine in his glass and watched the amber liquid catch the light, then said heavily, 'Maisie seemed a charming and attractive woman and we went out once or twice. Certainly I was attracted to her,' he confessed with a rueful grin. 'I also felt sorry for her as she told me her own father had died recently and he had been the only family she'd had.'

'So she made the first move?'

'And I wasn't too averse,' admitted Ronan. 'What happened was basically my fault. I could have said no, and I certainly wasn't thinking of a permanent relationship. We had little in common—I love the countryside and she was bored by Arrandale…'

A flicker of irritation darted through Lisa. 'So you led her on?' she said sarcastically.

'Perhaps I did, but it was certainly a lesson to me not to leap into a relationship and also to make sure the person you choose has a similar background and interests!'

Lisa flicked a look at the flinty expression on his face. The message was clear—Ronan wasn't interested in anyone who didn't come from his exclusive circle. He was implying in a not very subtle way that anyone from a different background would not fit into his life—in other words, he was a snob— a drop-dead gorgeous snob. A spark of anger flashed through her and she thought of the arrogance her mother had endured when she had been young from people who'd thought they were better than she was.

'So, did you bring your little liaison to an end when you realised that she wasn't "your sort"?' There was a cutting edge to Lisa's voice—her sympathies were still with Maisie at the moment.

Ronan frowned, then said firmly, 'I wasn't implying anything about differences in class—I hope I'm not that shallow. By background I meant her outlook on life really. When I realised that from my point of view we were going nowhere, I paid the money back myself and tried to finish our relationship.'

'But how come you became engaged if you didn't love her?'

His mouth tightened and he looked stonily at Lisa. 'Maisie's charming front fell away. She told me she was pregnant and that she would have an abortion if we didn't get married.'

Lisa's eyes widened. 'She blackmailed you? I can hardly believe she'd do that…she seemed so nice.'

'Charm is Maisie's stock in trade,' remarked Ronan drily. 'It took some time to realise that she's as hard as nails and when it comes to ambition. Nothing will stop her.'

Lisa looked puzzled and then said slowly, 'But you didn't get married to her anyway…'

The blue eyes darkened. 'I would have married her if it meant saving the baby,' he said intensely. 'It would have been my child as well—and I would have loved it totally. I had been wrong to have an affair with someone I didn't love but I would have put my all into the marriage if we'd had a baby to-gether—after all, the child comes first.'

He twirled the glass in his hand and looked across at her, the evening sun striking his sad face, and Lisa knew that he meant what he'd said.

'We all make mistakes,' she said in a softer tone.

His mouth tightened and he said harshly, 'But it was all a con—she knew she wasn't pregnant at all.'

'You found out she wasn't pregnant?'

'I became suspicious after a few weeks and insisted she have a blood test…then she admitted she never had been ex-pecting a baby.'

'So the relationship ended?'

'When I told her that it would be unfair to both of us to stay together she was very angry—made quite a few threats, followed me to see if I was seeing other women.' He gave a dry laugh and touched the white scar at the side of his mouth. 'I'll always have something to remind me of her…'

Lisa stared at him incredulously. 'She did that to you? What with?'

He grinned. 'I didn't duck quickly enough when she threw a handy kitchen knife at me…but that's all water under the bridge. I just hoped I'd never see the woman again—I didn't think she'd come back, like she did the other day.'

'I can't believe it,' Lisa said at last. 'She…she didn't look the sort to manipulate a relationship like that.' She looked across at him wide-eyed. 'And that's the whole story?'

'It's enough, isn't it?' he said, with some bitterness in his voice. 'My fault entirely. I encouraged Maisie when I didn't really love her—then I found out how calculating she could be in order to get a ring on her finger.' He paused for a minute then said softly, 'But you know something? Even though I didn't love Maisie, I mourned the baby we never had—I guess I wanted a child more than I realised. When I believed she was pregnant I felt real excitement, ready to take on a new role. It hit me like a sledgehammer to realise that she'd used her so-called pregnancy as a trap. I'll never be caught that way again,' he added grimly.

He stared unseeingly across the darkening garden, and Lisa was silent as she reflected that surely she of all people knew how one could be controlled against one's will, duped into doing things that one didn't really want to do. In that respect, her past was chillingly reminiscent of Ronan's. Looking across at him, she saw for the first time a wistfulness beneath the stern exterior, a hint of loneliness about the man.

'I'm very sorry Ronan,' she said at last, and reached out to touch his hand comfortingly. 'It was a despicable thing to do.'

His eyes were still dark with anger, but with an effort he managed a weak smile. 'Thank you,' he said gruffly. 'I made a mistake with Maisie—and then I made one with you, too, when I grabbed you the way I did, using you to get rid of her.'

'My mother used to say that the man who never makes a mistake never makes anything,' said Lisa crisply. She stood up quickly, all at once frightened of her swinging emotions, and gave a breathless laugh. 'You know something? I'm being eaten alive by midges—shall we go in?'

He slid his arm around her in a companionable way as they went inside, and it felt as if every nerve in her body was tingling as he drew her towards him and she felt the stride of his leg against hers. He stopped for a second and turned her towards him, holding her shoulders and looking down into her face.

'Thank you for listening. I've never really talked to anyone about the reason Maisie and I split up.'

Perhaps it was the wine or the fact that she no longer felt angry about him kissing her the other day, but when he put his finger under her chin and tilted her face to his, she didn't turn away when he brushed her forehead with his lips before they sat down. She looked across at him, his austere but good-looking features frowning slightly at the menu, and suddenly realised that what she really wanted wasn't food at all. Now she knew what it felt to be kissed by him, all she wanted was to feel his comforting arms around her again, the reassuring thud of his heart against hers and to feel his hands exploring every bit of her.

She wanted to tell him that she knew how desolate and alone he'd felt, trapped in an unhappy love affair—because that was what had happened to her. The plain fact was that she fancied Ronan like mad—more than any man she'd ever met before—and it wasn't just because he was so drop-dead gorgeous. He'd revealed an honesty about his shortcomings and a willingness to face up to his responsibilities that was an attractive facet of his character.

Ronan studied the menu without seeing any of the words, only aware of Lisa and how beautiful she'd looked as she'd listened to his pathetic tale. He couldn't believe how close he'd come just a minute ago to taking her in his arms again and kissing her properly, almost in gratitude at her sympathy and understanding. He flicked a covert glance at her, noting her flawless complexion, the way her eyelashes swept over her high cheekbones and the curve of her full breasts under the silk trouser suit. He took a deep breath. Was he making the same mistake again—confusing lust for love? He'd made a mess of his life once he thought grimly. He wasn't going to do it again.

'Are you as hungry as I am?' he asked almost brusquely.

'Of course,' she said brightly. But not for food exactly— the kind of hunger she was experiencing was to do with his mouth kissing hers, his body pressed to hers.

'Then let's start,' he said, signalling to the waiter that they were ready.

Lisa did her best with the steak and ale pie, but her appetite for food had gone. After all the months of anguish and the loneliness when her mother had died, she needed someone desperately—and she guessed he did, too. His affair with Maisie had been wrong, but it sounded as if Maisie hadn't really loved him either, just tried to trap him by one of the oldest tricks in the book, telling him she was pregnant.

Lisa finished her glass of wine and looked across at him speculatively, the alcohol subtly removing some of her inhibitions. She put her chin in her hands and smiled across at him. He grinned back at her, and it seemed to her his blue eyes were provocative, teasing.

'You look very relaxed,' he said.

'I've probably had too much to drink—good job you're driving. It's a lovely place this, Ronan. Thank you for the meal…'

'You haven't eaten much,' he commented.

'I'm really full. Should we better go now? I've got to pack up my things and move tomorrow morning, remember.'

'OK. I'll get the bill…'

Ronan got up and walked to the desk, his back view, broad and tall, as sexy as he was from the front, thought Lisa. She shook herself mentally, angry for forgetting the lessons she'd learned with Trevor and allowing herself to imagine the wonderful things Ronan might do to her if she let him! The truth was, she longed for him to kiss her again—and more!

CHAPTER FIVE

IT WAS pitch dark as they drove through the countryside co-cooned together in the car, Lisa watching Ronan's strong hands on the steering-wheel. It was idiotic, imprudent, everything that was foolish, but she wanted him to make love to her so much. Was she mad to feel this overpowering attraction for him, and did he feel anything at all for her?

He glanced across at her. 'A penny for your thoughts,' he said lightly.

'Oh…I was just thinking what a lovely meal it was…'

'You didn't seem to eat much. Are you feeling OK?'

She smiled faintly in the dark. She could hardly tell the truth—that she was beginning to realise that he meant more to her than any man, that she felt dizzy with desire and that her imagination was running riot!

'Of course I feel all right, although I've probably had too much alcohol…'

He laughed. 'You've only had a glass or two—probably just enough to make you feel sleepy.'

'I'm not tired at all—I feel full of energy,' she protested. And that was true—she felt as taut as a violin string, on edge, as if something momentous was going to happen.

He grinned, his teeth white in the half-light. 'If we were in London we'd go on to a club, I suppose,' he said. 'Somewhere with good music.'

'That would have been fun—I like music. I love to dance.'

He gazed steadily at the road before him, and his knuckles tightened slightly on the steering-wheel. 'I imagine you're a very good dancer... a pity there aren't many opportunities for that round Arrandale.'

It started to rain, heavy drops hissing against the windscreen, and Ronan turned on the windscreen-wipers, peering through the black night down the narrow road. On the skyline the hills looked dark and threatening, the clouds scudding over a half-moon through an angry sky.

'This weather's the pits,' he muttered, slowing down to a crawl as he came to a sharp corner. Then he made a sudden exclamation and shouted, 'Hell!'

Lisa was thrown forward as he jammed on the brakes and they planed across the waterlogged road, stopping inches away from a tangled mass of metal slewed across their path.

Lisa screamed and he looked across at her sharply. 'You OK?'

'Yes, I'm fine. It was just the shock...' She gave a quick intake of breath. 'My God,' she whispered in horror. 'What on earth's happened here? It looks terrible. Have you got a torch?'

'In the glove compartment. I'll put the hazard lights on— we don't want another car slamming into us. Come on, let's have a look.'

They scrambled out of the car, the full force of the rain hitting them so that in a few seconds they were both drenched. As they reached the wreckage, steam was hissing out of the twisted bonnet. Bizarrely, music was still thumping from the radio.

'Looks as if it's just happened,' shouted Ronan over the sound of the wind. He swept the beam of the torch over the wreckage and bent down to a crumpled door in the side of what had once been an expensive and powerful saloon.

'There's someone trapped in here,' he yelled. He tugged his mobile out of his trouser pocket and stabbed out some numbers. Above the noise of the rain and increasing wind Lisa could hear him yelling for an ambulance and emergency service back-up. She crouched down by his side and peered into the wrecked vehicle. A young man lay back in the driver's seat, his head back and blood oozing out of his nose. Another young man was slewed across him on the other side, a large purple bump on his forehead. Both were unconscious.

Lisa pushed her arm through the gash in the door and just managed to reach the man's neck and put her finger on his carotid artery.

'I can feel a pulse…he's alive,' she shouted at Ronan. 'What can we do?'

'Not much,' he said grimly. 'Until someone comes with cutting equipment, it'll be difficult to get them out without jolting them. We don't know what internal injuries they have, damage to the spinal cord perhaps.' Then he paused and swept his torch over the ground, bending down and investigating the area. He gave a quick intake of breath. 'Oh, my God, this is petrol—it's leaking all over the place.'

Lisa's heart started to thump with horror. 'Is it going to explode? We'll have to get them out, won't we?'

'We've no choice,' he shouted back. 'If the petrol touches hot metal, the whole thing could go up in flames. Hold the torch and let me see if I can shift any of this metal. I've got a pair of gloves in my car and a rug on the back seat. Can you get them?'

He pulled on the gloves she gave him with frantic haste and started to tug at the jagged edges of the door. It creaked and moved slightly.

'I might be able to do it,' he panted. 'I just need some more leverage…'

'Let me help—two of us might do better.'

Lisa tore off her jacket and put it over the metal and together they heaved and pulled. With a creaking, rending sound the edges of the door bent back.

'We'll have to try and get them out as gently as we can…don't know how possible that is,' grunted Ronan. 'This one's not got a safety belt on—if I pull him towards you, can you take the weight of his shoulders for a minute?'

Lisa gritted her teeth and with every ounce of strength she had took the man's full weight as Ronan tried to disengage the victim's legs from the tangled wreckage.

'Hurry, Ronan, This petrol's everywhere…'

He straightened up from the well of the vehicle and then put his arms round the man's body. 'I hope this isn't going to kill him,' he said grimly. 'Take his legs Lisa—now! Carefully does it. Can you hang on a little bit more and we'll put him behind these bushes?'

They staggered to the side of the road and lowered the man down as gently as they could, getting him as near to the bushes as possible to protect him from the rain and ensuring he wouldn't choke on his own vomit if he was sick.

'Quick! Come on—let's tackle the other one.'

They were too late. With a sickening whoosh and roar, a ball of flame billowed from the engine area. Lisa screamed,

putting her hands in front of her face in horror. With a muttered curse Ronan dived forward and pushed his way through
the enlarged gap in the side of the car.

'No, Ronan, no! Come back, you idiot…you'll be killed.
Don't do it!'

'Stand back!' she heard him yell as he disappeared. All she
could do was stay with the patient while watching the flames
engulf the front of the car. In that instant she knew that Ronan
meant far more to her than she'd ever imagined. How could
this have happened just as she'd realised how much she cared
for him? How could she lose him so quickly? A huge ragged
sob shook her, and tears coursed down her face.

Then, after what seemed minutes, she saw him reappear,
dragging a limp body with him. She gave a gasp of relief as
he staggered towards her and she sprang forward and grabbed
the man's legs. Together they managed to heave him away
from the heat of the burning car and as they laid him down
near his companion then there was a huge explosion as the rest
of the car went up. Ronan sank to the ground and put his head
between his knees, his breath coming in great ragged gasps.

'Are you all right? Are you burned?' Lisa crouched down beside him, turning his blackened, rain-streaked face towards her.

'No,' he croaked. 'Just winded…and exhausted. I'm fine.
Go back to your patient. This one's at least in better shape so
I'll stay with him.' He nodded at the second man who was
groaning and moving restlessly from side to side.

Lisa went back to the first man they'd got out of the car
and knelt down beside him, checking his vital signs. There
was a heartbeat—rather ragged, but still beating. His legs
looked badly damaged and when she spoke to him his eyes
fluttered slightly. She shone the torch in each eye to see his

pupil reaction, then looked more closely at his face. He was much younger than she'd thought.

'I know you!' she exclaimed. 'I've seen you before…' She racked her brains to find the elusive connection. She didn't know many people in this area—he had to be a patient. Then she suddenly remembered—a loud television set, a smoky room…

'Good God,' she breathed, 'it's Kevin MacCann…he's fourteen years old!'

She daren't move him any more and concentrated on supporting his head. It was impossible to tell what internal injuries he might have and the risk of exacerbating those was too great. At least both boys were out of the burning vehicle and both were alive. Faintly she heard the sound of a police siren and through the pouring rain she saw the most welcome sight of a flashing blue light. Thank God! She called to Ronan, who had turned away from his patient, coughing and spluttering to get rid of the smoke he'd inhaled.

'The ambulances are here, Ronan—it's OK.'

He nodded and got up from the ground gingerly, staggering slightly as he did so. A police car and two ambulances had pulled up, the rain looking like silver drops in the beams of their headlights. Several figures were running across to them.

'Can you tell me what happened?' asked one paramedic, his fluorescent jacket shining in the dark. He looked more closely at Ronan. 'It's Dr Gillespie, isn't it?'

Ronan nodded and quickly told the paramedics everything they needed to know as they began to treat the casualties.

'Any idea of their names, who they are?' asked the first paramedics.

'I recognise one of them,' said Lisa, pointing to Kevin

MacCann. 'That one—he's called Kevin MacCann. He's a patient of Dr Gillespie's.'

'Right, it all helps…'

A policeman arrived, a gabble of voices coming from the walkie-talkie clipped to his jacket. 'Ah, Dr Gillespie—lucky they had you on the scene. Did I hear you say that one of these lads is Kevin MacCann?' He sighed and said heavily, 'I'm not surprised, and I expect the other boy's his brother. This is a stolen car—I've run a check on the number plate that's just about still visible.'

'Let's hope they've not learned too harsh a lesson, then,' said Ronan grimly. He turned to Lisa. 'That metal has made a mess of your hands. I want you to go with this team and have them looked at.'

Lisa looked at him stubbornly. 'They're only cut—and my anti-tetanus shots are up to date. I'm not going to hospital to spend hours in Casualty—I'm perfectly all right. If anyone's going, it should be you.'

He grinned and gave a resigned shrug. 'Looks like it's a case of "physician, heal thyself" then. I'll look at your hands myself when I get back.'

The youths were stretchered into the ambulances, both with oxygen masks over their faces and portable drips inserted into their arms. The policeman came back from looking at the burnt-out wreck of the car.

'Perhaps you could give me a statement at the station tomorrow, sir—and you, too, miss.'

'This is Dr Balfour, my new colleague,' explained Ronan. 'Tomorrow morning I'm helping to move her into Bill Garrity's cottage by the loch, so could we come after that?'

The policeman nodded. 'No problem.' He looked them up

and down with an amused smile. 'I'm no doctor, but I'd say if you don't get home soon and into a hot bath, you might both get hypothermia.'

Lisa and Ronan looked at each other, dripping hair plastered to their heads and wringing wet clothes. 'Talk about drowned rats,' remarked Ronan. 'I think we'll do as you suggest, and dry off as quickly as possible.'

It was only as they were driving home that Lisa began to realise just how cold and shocked she was after the horror of the crash. Ronan gave a concerned glance across at her shivering body and chattering teeth. Reaction from the ghastly evening was beginning to set in.

'A pity the evening had to end like this, Lisa. I think a little hot toddy might get your circulation going again. Then we'll have a steaming bath and I'll look at those hands of yours.'

Lisa was completely exhausted, mentally and physically. She closed her eyes and leant back in the seat, trying to shut out the images of the terrible crash and feeling a dull sense of disappointment that the evening hadn't finished as she'd thought it would. Perhaps it was just as well, she reflected. She and Ronan…well, it would have been a silly thing for them to have got together anyway—the accident at least had stopped her making a pass at him that she would probably have regretted. The evening had only been meant to break the ice between them, not lead to a sexual encounter in any way, hadn't it?

The car stopped and Lisa stumbled out. Helped by Ronan, she managed to get to the front door. How wonderful to be inside the house—warm and comforting after the rigours of the evening. She flopped down onto a sofa in the hall and after a few minutes Ronan appeared with a glass of golden liquid.

'Here,' he said, handing her the glass, 'There's warm whisky and ginger wine in this—sip it slowly and then take off all those soaking clothes.' He swept a glance over her mud-spattered figure, the blue silk of her trouser suit ripped and stained. 'I don't think you'll be wearing that beautiful suit again,' he commented wryly.

Lisa shrugged. 'It doesn't matter. As long as those boys—and you—are safe.'

'I'll just go and get that bath going.'

After a short time he reappeared, this time dressed in an old dressing-gown.

'It'll have to be a shower,' he said angrily. 'I doubt there's enough hot water for a bath. Come on!'

He looked down at Lisa's shivering figure on the sofa and before she could protest that she was perfectly capable of getting up the stairs on her own, he had scooped her up in his arms and was pounding up the stairs.

'You're exhausted, aren't you?' he said briskly. 'The sooner you have that shower, the better!'

Ronan held her close to him and she could feel his heart thudding against his rib cage and the strength of his arms through the thin fabric of the dressing gown, and it seemed as if a thousand little butterflies were fluttering in her stomach. The warm whisky coursed through her body and she began to experience that gradual fading of inhibitions. She clung to him and put her cheek against the evening stubble of his jaw.

'Don't drop me,' she said, slightly slurred.

'As if I would.' he murmured.

He put her down gently in the bathroom and, bending beside her, took her cut hands in his, looking at them closely. Then he dabbed them gently, almost tenderly, with cotton wool soaked in disinfectant. 'Sorry about the stinging,' he said.

Lisa looked down at his bent head, the solicitous way he tended her hands—it had been a long time since a man had treated her so gently. A picture of Trevor's face flashed into her mind—good-looking, charming when he wanted to be, but cold and selfish. Ronan had a tough side to him but, unlike Trevor, he could be compassionate and kind. She'd almost forgotten how comforting it was to be looked after and cared for.

Ronan looked up at her mock sternly. 'Go on, then,' he urged. 'Have that shower quickly and then I'll have one.'

A mixture of sadness and loneliness engulfed Lisa. Perhaps it was the dramatic events of the evening and the subsequent kindness of Ronan, but the emptiness of the last few months suddenly overwhelmed her. In the whole world, who really cared about what happened to her? If she had been involved in that crash there would have been no family to help her— she was absolutely alone in the world. She needed to be soothed, she thought muzzily, have comforting arms wrapped around her, and it was as if the bizarre evening could only end one way. She looked him straight in the eye.

'There might not be enough hot water for two showers— you're just as cold as I am.'

There was a short silence and the sense of intimacy in the warmth of the bathroom increased—sparks of sexual attraction flickered tantalisingly between them.

Ronan raised a quizzical eyebrow. 'What are you saying?' he murmured, tilting her face to his. 'Do you mean it's better to have one long hot shower than two brief ones?'

He was so very close. She could smell the male smell of him, see the slight indentation of the dimple near his mouth, his damp hair standing in spikes round his forehead, a purpling bruise on his forehead from the accident.

'I…I mean you mustn't get cold waiting for me, must you?'

'Is that a medical assessment?'

She tried to smile, lighten her mood. 'Of course…it would be dangerous to risk lowering your core body temperature.' Then her voice became a whisper, so that Ronan had to bend forward to catch what she said. 'It's just. It's been a terrible night. I should be used to mangled bodies from working in Casualty…but I thought you'd been killed when you went into those flames…'

Suddenly tears began to pour down her face and she put her injured hands up to her mouth to hide her sobs.

His arms went around her and he held her to him, patting her back as one would a frightened child, soothing her with murmured words. 'Now, now, don't worry, sweetheart. This is just a reaction to the shock of the evening. You did so well, helping me get that lad out of the car. No wonder you're in shock—just relax now.'

Gradually Lisa became calmer and she relaxed against Ronan, feeling the steady throb of his heart beating against hers. Then she wound her arms around him and pulled his head down, brushing her lips against his firm mouth.

'Thank you,' she whispered. 'This is just what I need.'

He gave a shudder and put his hands on the lapels of her jacket, his clear blue eyes questioning hers. 'Are we playing a dangerous game here, Lisa?' he said huskily, then he kissed her back gently.

'It's been a strange evening. I…I find this very comforting…'

It was madness, she knew, and she was taking things too fast, leading the way—but what the hell? She couldn't help herself. She was shocked, lonely and emotionally fragile—and it had been so long since anyone had shown her affection. She stood up and undid the buttons on her jacket and shrugged it off, wriggling out of the trousers so that they slipped like a pool of blue to the floor, and she stood naked before him. His eyes swept over her slim, full-breasted body and he drew a deep breath.

'You're not making it easy to resist you, Lisa,' he said softly. 'Is this part of the treatment for shattered nerves?'

She laughed shakily. 'It could help…'

He made no reply, but flung off his dressing-gown and drew their naked bodies together for a minute before taking her hand and leading her into the shower.

He turned on the shower taps so that stinging needles of hot water sprayed over them. Then he wrapped his arms about her and bent his head to hers, kissing her wet face, her neck and her soft breasts, his naked body pressed to hers.

'My God,' he breathed huskily. 'Is this wonderful, or what?'

She bent back her head and sighed as his mouth traced a series of soft kisses down her neck and her slippery body slid against his. He turned off the taps as the water became cooler and reached out for a towel, wrapping it around her as they both stepped out of the cubicle. Lisa's legs felt shaky, her whole body trembling with desire, a yearning for him to make love to her.

He looked down at her gravely. 'This isn't how I thought the evening would end, but now it looks like the moment of no return, you know. If this is all you want, say so now.'

'No,' she whispered, her eyes closed and swaying slightly. 'It isn't all I want… I don't want it to end now…'

'Then that's all right.' His amazing blue eyes looked into hers. 'You see, I don't want it to end either.'

He gathered her up in his arms again and took her to his bedroom, putting her down on his huge old-fashioned four-poster bed. He lay on top of her, his face pale in the meagre night light from the window, then he bent his head and covered her with butterfly kisses, trailing his lips softly over the little hollow in her neck. In that moment she forgot the sadness of the past and gave herself up to the undiluted pleasure of the present.

Later, Lisa lay awake in the dark, listening to Ronan quietly breathing beside her, his body wrapped around hers, and a flicker of shame darted through her. Had she just made the biggest mistake of her life, making love to someone she suspected would not want a permanent relationship, using him because she felt sorry for herself?

'Too late to worry about that now,' she murmured, 'Because I've fallen hook line and sinker for Ronan anyway.'

Then she drifted off into a deep exhausted sleep.

And now it was the morning. Brilliant sunshine filtered through the curtains and warmed Lisa's face so that she stirred momentarily.

'Tea for your ladyship?'

Ronan's deep voice broke through her dreams and she opened her eyes to see his tall figure looking down at her from beside the bed, a tray in his hands. For a second she looked up at him blankly, wondering where she was. Then it all flooded back to her—the horror of the accident and then their love-making the night before—and how indisputably to her shame she had led him on.

She sat up quickly, then realised she had nothing on at all and drew the sheet up to her chin protectively.

'A bit late for modesty now.' Ronan grinned, sitting on the bed and putting a steaming cup of tea on the little bedside table. His hand reached out and brushed the hair from her forehead. 'Have you recovered from last night?'

She looked at him warily, her thoughts spinning in confusion around her head. Last night she'd realised that there was no going back as far as she was concerned—she'd fallen for Ronan in a big way, wanted him to make love to her, to comfort her. But she wasn't going to sound too enthusiastic, let him know that it had been wonderful, heart-stoppingly fantastic. For him it had probably been a reaction to the evening's drama and meant nothing more to him than his affair with Maisie had done. And in any case, she thought dully, how could she measure up to him? Their backgrounds were so different—poles apart. They could have come from different universes.

She smiled at him brightly. 'It…it was fun—at least the last part of the evening was!'

Ronan frowned slightly and raised one eyebrow. 'Just fun? A little romp, is that all?' His mouth twisted in a wry smile. 'You seemed to enjoy it, though!'

'Of course…' Lisa took a sip of tea, the colour rising in her cheeks, and she looked down, too embarrassed to show the naked longing in her eyes. 'Of course I enjoyed it.'

He got up from the bed and leant against the door lintel, his intelligent eyes looking down at her with a slightly puzzled expression. 'I thought it might have meant more to you than that,' he said rather flatly. He shrugged and looked at his watch. 'And now it's off to Bill Garrity's when you're ready.'

'I won't take long.'

'Lisa…' He paused for a second, looking at her carefully

as if gauging her reaction to his words. 'You don't have to leave, you know. You can stay here as long as you want..'

'I must go,' Lisa replied simply. 'I've enjoyed your hospitality long enough. It was only supposed to be a short-term arrangement…and anyway,' she added, 'you didn't really want me to stay with you at first, did you?'

Ronan shrugged. 'I was taken aback when my sister suggested it. After all, I'd only met you before very briefly and we might not have hit it off. It could have been difficult, living and working together, having no personal space…'

He came back to the bed again and drew up a chair, sitting close beside her. He took her hands gently in his. 'But now I don't want you to go,' he said gruffly. 'Anyway, what's all this about? Are you getting cold feet? I can't believe that last night meant nothing more to you than a one-off. You're not that kind of girl.'

Lisa swallowed hard, her throat tight. 'Of course it meant a lot,' she said tersely. 'But living under the same roof and having a casual affair? I think not. Perhaps we were hasty.'

A casual affair—was that what he wanted? Ronan sighed. He'd made one mistake and he didn't want to make another, but in his heart of hearts he knew that a casual affair and Lisa wouldn't work. He flicked a glance at her face and saw to his shock bright unshed tears in her eyes.

'I think there was more to you leaving Grangeford than you told me,' he said gently. 'I've told you about my past life—perhaps you should tell me about yours.'

He handed her a handkerchief and she blew her nose and wiped her eyes, half laughing in embarrassment and at how shrewdly he'd read her emotions. 'Everyone has a history,' she remarked lightly. 'But I'm not going into that now. Look, I'm going to get dressed and you can help me take my stuff to the cottage. I'll be down in a minute.'

When Ronan went out, she sat for a second, leaning back against the pillows, gazing blankly out of the window. He had been kind to her—and understanding—but there was no way she could go into the complications behind her move to Arrandale at the moment. It would, she thought glumly, take a whole day to explain. She had to get away from him before things became too complicated—every night she spent in his house would make it more difficult to leave. The embarrassing thing was that she had made all the running last night—she had no one to blame but herself if it ended in tears.

Ronan sat down in the kitchen, waiting for Lisa to appear, absent-mindedly stroking Tam's head as the dog nuzzled his nose into his master's lap, hoping for a walk. It was Sod's law, he thought with bitter amusement, that now he'd met a woman to whom he felt more attracted than anyone he'd met before, she should start backpedalling. She'd seemed so happy last night when they'd made love, as eager as he had been—but this morning she'd changed. For a few seconds Lisa had revealed her private heartache, and perhaps until she came to terms with her past she would never commit herself to anyone. And that was an irony—because he was wary of doing that as well.

He got up and clicked his fingers for Tam to follow him as he went outside. There were a lot of questions he needed to ask Lisa, and he intended to find out the answers as soon as he could.

CHAPTER SIX

THERE wasn't much to pack in Ronan's large car, reflected Lisa, not much to show for a few years of work in Grangeford—just some books and a few small things of her mother's. It was as if she had never truly belonged anywhere before. And yet as they drove up to the little cottage by the loch she looked round with a small flicker of excitement. Surely here she could put down roots and become part of the community as she never had in Grangeford. After all, she had more connections with this part of the world than she'd ever had there. And half-guiltily she had to admit that as her mother had died she could now live for herself, do what she wanted to do without reference to anyone else, have freedom to make her own choices.

Lisa looked across at Ronan's serious face as he drove the car down the little unmade road to the cottage, flicked a glance at his strong hands on the wheel, hands that only a few hours ago had caressed her so intimately in heady passion. He was everything she wanted, but how much commitment would she get from this man? After all, he had confessed he'd started an affair with a woman merely because of physical attraction, and had finished it because they'd had such dissimilar 'backgrounds and interests'. Oil and water don't mix, she told herself wistfully. Would he view *her* upbringing as an obstacle to their relationship? Perhaps she was being silly. Surely she knew enough about Ronan to know he wasn't as shallow as that. And yet it was a risk, and she didn't want to be hurt again. It was right to leave his house and get him out of her mind completely.

A little wooden jetty ran out from the shingle and moored alongside it a small rowing boat bobbed in the water. Bill Garrity's cottage was part of a terrace of white cottages, each with a neat row of palings in front of a small garden. As Ronan parked the car, several children were kicking a football around on the strip of grass that ran in front of the shoreline. There was a lot of shrieking and laughter as they tried to score in a makeshift goal and then a groan as the ball missed and came hurtling towards Ronan and Lisa.

Ronan put out an adroit foot, stopped the ball and started to dribble it mischievously away from the children. They ran after him, shouting, 'Dr Gillespie, kick it back here—go on!'

He ran back towards the goal, looking like the Pied Piper of Hamlyn, with the children following him, and when he kicked it into the goal they gave a cheer. He looked so happy and at ease with them, reflected Lisa. He was having fun and so were they. There was no doubt, Lisa thought wistfully, that Ronan would make a wonderful father. There was no doubt that he enjoyed the company of children.

'Pretty impressive,' she remarked as he ran up to her. 'You ought to form a youth team.'

He smiled. 'That's not a bad idea. If I had more time, I might do that.'

A woman appeared at the door of one of the cottages and shouted at one of the children to come in, then, seeing Lisa and Ronan, walked over to them.

'Good morning, Ronan,' she called. 'I knew someone had taken Bill's house but I didn't realise you'd be moving today. I just hope that these young tearaways don't make too much noise…'

'Hello, Mary. Can I introduce Lisa Balfour, my new partner in the practice? This is Mary Lovat, Lisa. Her husband Danny is in charge of the fishing on the Carstairs' estate.'

'Welcome to the White Cottages.' Mary smiled. 'If you need any help, do ask me.'

'You're very kind. I'm really looking forward to living here.' Lisa looked around at the loch and the sweeping shoreline. 'This is all part of the Carstairs' estate, then?'

'Sure. You can see the big house he lives in through the trees to the side of the loch.'

Lisa stared in fascination at the beautiful Victorian house built of golden stone. Her mother would have known that house so well, probably played and swum in the loch as a child, run past these very cottages…

'It's a lovely place,' she commented. 'I wonder what it's like inside?'

'You can find out next month if you like—there's to be a big coffee morning in aid of the nursing home,' said Mary.

'Not another one,' groaned Ronan. 'I suppose Richard's trying to salve his conscience by being seen to do something for the nursing home?'

Mary shook her head reprovingly. 'Ah, come on, he's a kind man, and to be fair he's been getting a pittance from the council for the lease of the building. I shall expect you to be there,' she said sternly to Ronan. Then she turned to Lisa. 'Talking of coffee, why don't you both come and have one now with me?'

'I'm so sorry—perhaps another time,' said Lisa regretfully. 'We've got to go to the police station to give a statement about a traffic accident last night.'

Mary's eyes widened. 'You were there, were you? The accident on the Inverleith Road? Wasn't young Kevin MacCann involved?'

'Not only Kevin, but his brother Neil as well,' remarked Ronan. 'I shall be finding out how he is later on today. He was lucky not to be killed.'

Mary looked at them critically. 'I can see now that you've been hurt, Ronan. That's a terrible bang you've got on your head. And your hands are all bandaged, Lisa. What a night you must have had—you must be exhausted, the two of you.'

Lisa felt her face redden and bent down to stroke the Lovats' cat on the path—she didn't need reminding what a night they'd had!

'It was an evening I certainly won't forget in a hurry—but at least it ended well,' said Ronan softly. His eyes flicked towards Lisa's, holding her gaze for a split second. Then he added smoothly, 'Neither boy lost his life, and hopefully no long-term damage has been done.' He opened the boot of the car and lifted out a large box. 'We'd better start moving Lisa's stuff now. We'll see you soon Mary.'

Inside, the cottage was much lighter than one would have supposed. A huge picture window in the small living room overlooked the magnificent view of loch and mountains beyond. Lisa watched a flock of ducks land on the water, their legs planing on the surface for all the world like miniature amphibious aircraft, and drifting far across the loch was a small yacht with white sails. There was a sense of peace and tranquillity about the place, despite the sounds of the children playing on the grass.

'I feel as if I'm home now,' whispered Lisa. 'As if I really belong.'

Ronan had taken her suitcases upstairs and stood looking at her in the doorway. Through the wide window the sunlight framed Lisa's profile in a pale light, emphasising her slim silhouette, making her golden hair seem like a halo. He waited for a moment, then went over to her and put his hand lightly on her shoulder, looking out with her at the view. She moved slightly away from his touch sending, she hoped, a subtle message that they should keep their distance.

He dropped his hand and said quietly, 'I'm glad you feel part of the place. I want you to be happy here.'

'I know I will be—and you're right about me feeling part of the place. You see, I'm sure this is probably where my mother played as a young child. She loved it and because she did, I do too.'

Ronan looked at Lisa curiously. 'That intrigues me,' he said. 'If your mother had such a happy childhood here, why did she never come back?'

'Money was scarce and so holidays were out of the question.' She looked at him almost proudly. 'I was brought up in quite a hard school—no frills.'

'She was widowed, then?'

'I never knew my father. I just wish,' she said wistfully, 'that I'd brought Mum back to see Arrandale before she died. It's sad that she set her face against returning. I mean, just look at that view of the loch and the mountains behind—she must have missed that.'

'I don't want to pry, but what prevented her?'

Lisa gave a short laugh. 'Seems silly now—today nobody would condemn her at all for what happened—but, you see, for a long time she kept it a secret, not wanting to make me feel guilty that I was the reason that caused her to leave…'

Ronan frowned and leaned against a table, folding his arms. 'Why should you have felt guilty?'

'She became pregnant with me when she was still at school and only sixteen,' explained Lisa bluntly. 'In those days, having a baby without being married was looked on very harshly in a small community…'

A nod of understanding from Ronan. 'They gave her a bad time, then?'

'Her family were terrible to her.' Lisa voiced hardened as she told the story. 'In fact, they were downright cruel. She was only a young girl but they disowned her and sent her off to a mother and baby home in Grangeford, and the man who was my father disappeared very quickly. She never came back here again.'

There was silence for a second, the sound of a curlew's mewing floating through the open window, then Ronan said gently, 'That's a very sad story. I don't know how anyone could do that to their child, but I know it used to happen a lot. How did she manage?'

'She was great—full of courage and very independent,' said Lisa proudly. 'Because of her experience she was determined that I should be able to stand on my own feet and get some qualifications, whatever it cost her. She sacrificed everything for me…'

'So that's where you got your feisty nature,' Ronan remarked with a grin. 'Your mother never met anyone else, then?'

Lisa laughed. 'I'm afraid she never trusted men, although she called herself Mrs Balfour, using her middle name because she thought it would be easier for me.'

'It's none of my business,' Ronan said delicately, 'but who were the family—would I know them?'

'Their name was Carstairs…'

'Carstairs? As in the owner of Corrie House Nursing Home?' His blue eyes were wide with surprise.

'I think it's the same family—I know she mentioned Glenside House and playing there as a child. Mind you, I don't imagine Richard Carstairs knows anything about it.' Lisa looked at Ronan with a slight smile. 'So now you know why Arrandale has always held a fascination for me and why, although I don't want to bother the Carstairs in any way, I feel I have roots in the area.'

'So that's the reason you left Grangeford when your mother died?'

Lisa got up abruptly from the window-sill she'd been sitting on and walked briskly across the floor, then she turned to face him, her cheeks slightly flushed. 'No, that wasn't the reason I left Grangeford,' she said rather haltingly. 'There were things that happened there…that meant I couldn't stay in the place. But I chose to come to Arrandale because of my mother's roots here.'

She picked up her handbag from a small table. 'And now,' she said briskly, 'perhaps we'd better go and give our statements to the police, don't you think?'

He nodded, accepting her change of subject. 'I wonder if you'd mind dropping in to see Terry Newman, our injured partner, after we've been to the police station? He and his wife are dying to meet you, and now he's back from recuperating at his brother's while Lorainne was away. They're hoping we'll have some lunch with them.'

Was it wise to spend more time alone with Ronan? Certainly not, said a small voice inside Lisa's head. And yet she still had to work with the man—there was no point in being churlish just because she was frightened of getting too close to him. It wasn't his fault they'd made love the night before—she'd encouraged him every step of the way!

'Yes, I think Terry and I should meet—it's a good idea,' she agreed.

Despite her plans to spend time apart from Ronan, it seemed to Lisa that she was going to be with him for several hours yet!

They went to the police station and also rang up the hospital to discover how the two boys involved in the accident were. Apparently Kevin had fractured both legs and sustained a crush injury to his chest, and his brother was severely concussed and had a whiplash injury to his neck.

'The MacCann family have a lot of problems,' remarked Ronan as they drove to the Newmans'. 'The father is out of work and spends too much time in the pub, and Jean can match him when it comes to drinking. Those two young boys are disasters waiting to happen.'

'They've been in trouble before, then?'

'They have. I reckon the minor crime wave round the estate will abate for a few weeks while they recover from their injuries!' He turned the car off the road and into a short drive with fields on either side of it, and gave a deep sigh. 'And now let's forget about those lads and get some strong coffee!'

The Newmans lived outside the village in an old farm-house, the stone walls covered with a prolific pink climbing rose. One child was clambering over a climbing-frame and an-other was swinging on a rope hung from a tree. When they saw Ronan and Lisa they ran across the lawn shrieking with delight, jumping round him like small eager puppies.

'Uncle Ronan! Mummy said you were coming. We want you to meet our new rabbit—he's called Spot. Come on!'

Ronan put his hands up and laughed. 'In a minute. Let's say hello to your parents first.'

The little girl, rather plump with two little plaits sticking out on either side of her head, stared at Lisa critically. 'You've got pretty hair, hasn't she, Uncle Ronan?'

Lisa felt herself blush slightly at Ronan's amused glance. 'It certainly is pretty—a lovely colour, Suzy,' he said gravely.

Suzy turned to Lisa. 'Are you Uncle Ronan's girlfriend?' she asked.

'No, I'm not, I just work with him,' explained Lisa with a light laugh, avoiding Ronan's eye.

The other child, a small boy, frowned. 'Mummy's always trying to get a wife for Uncle Ronan—she says he's too darn fussy!'

Ronan raised his eyebrows. 'And I say you're too darned nosy, Ben! Now, go and tell Mummy we're here.'

They raced off round the back and soon the front door was opened by a tall woman wearing old jeans and a fleece.

'Ah, Ronan, great to see you. I was just cleaning out the rab-bit's run—so much for the children doing the work!' She turned to Lisa. 'We're so glad you've come to work here, and I'm really pleased to meet you. Terry's been worried sick about Ronan doing all the work. Come in and have some lunch.'

'Coffee will do fine, Lorainne…'

'Nonsense! There's not much but we're all eating so you must, too.'

The little girl took her mother's hand as they walked through the house and in a stage whisper said, 'That woman's not Uncle Ronan's girlfriend, you know, but perhaps you can get them together.'

Lorainne looked back and winked at them before turning back to her daughter. 'Suzy! It's rude to discuss people in front of them. Run along and tell Daddy that Ronan and Lisa are here while I bring in the sandwiches. Sorry about that.' She chuckled. 'Not the most tactful of children, I'm afraid.'

'Can I help you?' asked Lisa, following Lorainne into the kitchen.

'Thanks. Perhaps you could take this coffee through and I'll bring the sandwiches.' She smiled rather wearily at Lisa. 'I'm really disorganised. It's been non-stop since our oldest son got back from India a few weeks ago. I've been sorting him out for college, and then my mother became ill and I had to go and look after her. That's why Terry and the children went to his brother's to give me a break—my dear sister-in-law has been looking after both him and Ben and Suzy!'

'Where's my blue jacket, Mum?'

A tall, thin teenager came into the kitchen wearing torn jeans and a batik shirt, open to the waist. He flung himself down on a chair and sat back with his long legs spread out in front of him.

'Harry, before you collapse on a chair, this is Dad's new partner, Lisa Balfour. And, no, I don't know where your jacket is—where you dropped it, I suppose.'

Harry rose from the chair and put out a thin, knobbly hand

to shake Lisa's. He had a freckled face like his mother's and tousled fair hair. He grinned at her and helped himself to some crisps on the table, offering some to Lisa.

'Hope you know what you're taking on with Ronan and Dad—they work all the hours heaven sends!'

'I hope they can have some time off, then, now I'm here.' Lisa smiled. 'I believe you've just come back from India?'

'Yup. I was on a VSO scheme. I did all the paperwork, made sure people got their jabs and so on,' he explained. 'It was great—can't wait to go back.'

'I hope it won't be for some time,' said Lorainne. 'He's been under the weather for ages—that trip really took it out of him.'

'Oh, *Mum*! I'm fine! Mum's always fussing,' he said to an amused Lisa. 'I had a dose of Delhi belly on the day I got back. Not something I'd recommend on a plane, by the way. What with that and jet-lag, it's made me feel a bit odd.'

'How long have you been back?' asked Lisa.

'About two months now. I'm off to college next week.'

'You should have been feeling better by now,' observed Lisa. 'You do look very pale…'

'And have you seen how thin he is?' demanded Lorainne. 'There's not a spare ounce of flesh on him anywhere!'

'I thought the big epidemic in this part of the world is obesity,' growled Harry.

'Have you had any tests?' enquired Lisa.

'I've had loads of tests,' he groaned. 'Nothing's shown up. Dad thought I might have been infected by giardiasis—he says that's quite a common parasite—but I'm OK.'

'What about tests for malaria?'

'Had them ages ago—came back negative.'

Lorainne sighed. 'Terry's been at his brother's so he's not seen Harry for any length of time. Perhaps now he's back he'll get Harry sorted before he goes to college.' She looked at her watch. 'Hadn't you better be making tracks, Harry? I thought you were on duty this afternoon?'

'What do you do?' asked Lisa with interest.

'It's just a holiday job, stacking shelves in the supermarket in the village. I suppose I'd better get going. Have you got any aspirin, Mum, before I go? I've got a throbbing head.'

Loraine looked at him sharply. 'You feeling bad again? There you are! It's just not like you, Harry—have you got a temperature again?'

Harry pulled a face and said irritably, 'I'm OK! It's just a little headache—probably a hangover from last night. I'm off anyway.' He gave a sheepish grin to Lisa, as if apologising for his irritation. 'Nice to meet you, Lisa. See you later!'

They heard him bang the front door behind him and Lisa could see his back view cycling down the drive through the window.

'He's a lovely boy,' she said to Lorainne. 'You must be very proud of him.'

'He's not a bad kid—works hard and wanted to do his bit, doing voluntary work on his year out,' admitted Loraine. 'I'm just a bit concerned. He's one of those lucky ones who's never ill—it's so unlike him to have any symptoms. But as he said, he's had loads of tests, all negative, so I suppose I should stop worrying.'

Lisa followed Lorainne as they went into the lounge with the sandwiches and coffee and wondered uneasily if Lorainne had cause to worry. The boy was incredibly thin and pale—

and sometimes tests weren't always accurate. Perhaps she would have a word with Ronan later about him.

Terry was sitting on a couch with his leg up on a stool, the limb locked into position by an external metal frame. He was a big man with a genial ruddy face and humorous eyes.

'I'm so glad to meet you,' he said heartily, 'but sorry it has to be when I look like a beached whale. You can see why a big fellow like me could get a compound fracture if I fell awkwardly. I've promised Ronan and Lorainne I won't go skiing again!'

'It looks as if it was a pretty bad break,' commented Lisa. 'How did you do that?'

'I was a little optimistic—went ski-ing down a black run when I'm barely a blue run man. It left me with an unstable compound fracture of the tibia,' Terry explained ruefully. 'I hope to have the thing off next week and a cast put on instead. Then I'll be coming back to work.'

'We'll think about that. I'm not having you back until you have a note from your surgeon,' growled Ronan.

It was a pleasant lunch. Terry and Lorainne were good company and the children were bright and amusing. A lovely family, reflected Lisa, watching as the children flew around the garden on their bikes—the kind of family she'd dreamed of being part of when she'd been a child.

As if reading her thoughts, Terry's voice boomed out, 'And do you have a family nearby? Is that why you came to this part of the world?'

'My mother was born here but I don't know anyone yet...'

'We'll soon remedy that,' said Terry cheerfully.

'Of course we will,' agreed Lorainne. She smiled at Lisa. 'I don't suppose you could help out at the coffee morning in about four weeks' time at the Carstairs' house? It would be a good way to meet people. It's in aid of Corrie House, the nursing home outside Arrandale.'

Ronan laughed. 'Mary Lovat's already told us to be there. I reckon the supermarket's done a roaring trade in coffee recently!'

'I'd love to help,' said Lisa. 'I'm dying to see inside the Carstairs' house anyway—it looks gorgeous and I know my mother used to play there as a child.'

'Then that's a deal,' said Lorainne, breaking off as the phone rang in the hall. 'Won't be a minute,' she said as she went to answer it.

Ronan got up from his chair. 'We must go,' he said to Terry. 'I'll come in next week—and don't think of coming back until you've had the all-clear. Lisa and I can manage fine.'

'That's what I'm frightened of.' Terry grinned. 'Soon you won't need me at all!'

Lorainne came back to the room, looking worried and twisting her hands together nervously. 'That was the supermarket,' she said. 'Harry's not well. They say he's vomiting and shaking like a leaf. I just *know* there's something wrong with him, whatever the tests show. I'll go and get him now.'

'You stay here,' said Ronan firmly. 'Lisa and I will go— we'll be able to assess the situation firsthand. We'll ring you immediately we've seen him.'

As Ronan drove the car out of the drive, Lisa filled him in on what Lorainne had told her about Harry's health, and the fact that all the tests since he'd been in India had been negative.

'I don't think we should place a lot of reliance on those tests,' she added grimly. 'When he set out for work I didn't think he looked at all well.'

Ronan nodded. 'From what you tell me, there's something

running around his system that needs to be diagnosed as soon as possible.'

He roared into the supermarket car park and screamed to a halt, scattering pebbles behind him, and they both jumped out of the car.

CHAPTER SEVEN

THE first thing Ronan and Lisa heard as they walked into the manager's office was banging—the banging of a couch against the wall caused by the shaking of Harry's body. He lay back on the couch with fluttering eyes sunk into dark eye sockets, his teeth chattering. He looked very very ill.

The manager, a short stout man with pale blue eyes behind pebble-lensed glasses, stood nervously twisting his hands together beside the couch, and an equally nervous female assistant was standing with some rugs in her arms. They looked up anxiously when Ronan and Lisa came in.

'Are you Harry's parents?' the manager asked.

'No, we're doctor friends of the Newmans and we happened to be there when you called to say that Harry wasn't well.'

'I'm really glad to see you,' the manager exclaimed fervently, the words tumbling out in a breathless rush. 'The poor lad's in a bad way. We didn't know there was anything wrong with him until there was a terrible crash in the middle aisle, and all the tins Harry had been stacking rolled onto the floor as he fell across them.' He pointed to the girl. 'Janet found him, and he didn't seem too bad at first, but he's deteriorated in the last few minutes.'

'It's OK,' said Ronan briskly. 'We'll take over now—don't worry. I'm sure you've done all the right things…'

The manager and his assistant looked visibly relieved. Lisa was well aware of the calming effect a doctor with Ronan's confident personality had on a traumatic situation when he entered a room.

She put a hand on Harry's forehead. 'He's very chilled,' she murmured to Ronan.

'I…I feel so cold,' Harry whispered. 'I can't breathe…'

Her eyes met Ronan's and he took out his mobile phone. 'We're not wasting any time,' he said briskly. 'You need to get to hospital as quickly as possible, Harry—I'm sure you've got malaria. I'm ringing Inverleith Hospital to warn them we're on our way…'

The boy turned restlessly, his voice faint and slightly slurred. 'But the tests were negative and I've been back for weeks now…'

'We'll have some more tests done. I don't know what's been masking it, but occasionally it does take some time for the disease to become fully active.'

Lisa had brought in Ronan's medical bag from his car and was using a sphygmomanometer to take the boy's blood pressure. 'His BP's very low,' she murmured to Ronan. 'Under 60 over 80…'

Ronan turned to the manager. 'I'm not waiting for an ambulance,' he said. 'It'll take too long to get here. We'll take him in my car. Lisa, you sit in the back with him and perhaps three strong members of staff can carry him out—one taking his shoulders, one his hips and one his legs—as quickly as you can, please.'

The manager scuttled out to get help as Ronan snapped some information down the phone.

'They'll be ready for us,' he told Lisa. 'The Department of Tropical medicine in Glasgow will advise them and that will speed up diagnosis and treatment considerably. I've also rung the police and told them we want an escort to the hospital. Come on! Let's go!'

After a nightmare journey along the main road to Inverleith with a police car in front of them, its light flashing, they got Harry to the hospital. By this time he was virtually unconscious. He was taken through quickly to Intensive Care and after a short time the registrar, a large woman with a bustling manner, appeared.

'Good to see you, Ronan,' she said, holding out her hand to the two doctors. 'I'm Carol Jones,' she added, speaking to Lisa. 'I believe you've joined the practice in Arrandale? Just come into the office for a minute while I update you on Harry Newman.'

She continued briskly in the privacy of the office. 'First, good job you got Harry here as quickly as you did—he's suffering from acute respiratory failure, but he's on a ventilator now. We've taken bloods to do various tests—but I'm 99 per cent sure we're looking at malaria. He's just experienced the first stage of rigor and cold and he seems to be entering the next stage of high temperature.'

'So what are his chances?' asked Ronan grimly.

'The main risk is organ failure, but hopefully this isn't the strain where we're talking major problems with all the blood cells affected. That type doesn't normally go through the stages Harry's experiencing.'

'It sounds pretty hairy—let's hope his youth helps him. I think he's been a fairly fit young man.'

'We'd better let his parents know,' said Lisa. 'They must be worried sick.'

'I'll speak to them,' said the registrar. 'I know Terry Newman and I'll try and reassure him that Harry's getting the best care possible. Can you come back in an hour? I'll be able to give you more details then.'

'We'll go and have a coffee,' suggested Ronan. 'No point in going home yet.'

As they walked to the cafeteria Lisa said, 'It's a bit unusual this should happen after two or three months. I thought the incubation period for malaria was five to ten days.'

'Perhaps Carol will shed some light on that—I just hope the boy's going to be OK.'

They sat down in the cafeteria and watched the diverse selection of people who made up a hospital's population milling around them, then Lisa sighed.

'And to think I once thought that a country practice would be quiet and stress-free! In the past twenty-four hours we've attended two medical emergencies and the weekend isn't over yet!'

'What did I tell you?' said Ronan. 'Is this on a par with Grangeford?'

For the first time she laughed at the mention of her old life. 'Oh, we had emergencies then all right!' She sighed. 'It must be such a worry for the Newmans, this business with their son. They seem really nice people.'

Ronan nodded. 'They are—and Terry's a great doctor. As friends we go back a long way—he wanted to have a career in A and E and he would have been a consultant in no time.'

'So why didn't he?' asked Lisa.

'The usual—he got married and then had children. He just couldn't combine that branch of medicine with a family.' He smiled. 'Lorainne and he got married very young and then were trapped by a honeymoon baby, which scuppered their plans. Anyway, luckily for us he decided to become a GP instead—and he's wonderful.'

Lisa looked at him curiously. He'd used that word 'trapped' before when talking about babies. Of course, the first time had been when Maisie had told him a lie about her pregnancy—as he'd said, trying to trap him into marriage. Not quite the same thing as thwarting someone's career ambitions but nevertheless, as much as he seemed to like children, perhaps he regarded them as an impediment, not an asset!

They talked in a desultory way for a while, then Ronan said quietly, 'You look exhausted, Lisa. Why don't you take my car and go home? There's no need for us both to stay here. I'll get a taxi back.'

Lisa shook her head. 'I'm not going until I hear more about Harry—we should know soon.'

Sure enough, at that point Carol came marching towards their table and sat down with them.

'I thought you'd be in here,' she said. 'Just to tell you that Harry's got a strain of malaria called *Plasmodium vivax*—normally not too malignant a strain.'

'Why is he so ill, then?' asked Lisa.

'I think it's due to one or two factors,' explained Carol. 'The diarrhoea he got with the Delhi belly he suffered on the way home probably prevented his body absorbing the prophylactics—I think he was taking chloroquine, which he continued taking for about four weeks after his return.'

'Perhaps they then suppressed the symptoms even though the malaria had entered his bloodstream?' suggested Ronan.

'That's very possible—but because of the delay in diagnosis with false blood readings it's certainly become more serious.'

Lisa blew her cheeks out. 'Wow, he could have gone to college before he found out. What's the treatment now?'

'He'll be in ICU for a few days, and on the advice of the Tropical Disease Department we'll probably give him primaquine to eradicate parasites in the liver. At the moment we're just assessing whether he should have a blood transfusion or not.'

'Have you spoken to Terry?'

'I have, and he and Lorainne are coming over as soon as their babysitter arrives.'

'Then we'll be off,' said Ronan, getting out of his chair. 'The Newmans will want to talk to you and I'll catch up with them later.'

They walked out to the car park and got into Ronan's car.

'Quite a twenty-four hours, wasn't it?' he said, looking across at her.

'Yes,' she answered in a small voice. 'So many things have happened I feel…'

'Bewildered?' he supplied quietly. 'It's been a bit of a roller-coaster, I know, Lisa—and not just with medical scenarios.' His eyes sought hers, deep blue sexy eyes making her heart quiver.

She took a deep breath and said huskily, 'I never thought things would…well, go as fast as they did. I shouldn't have given you those signals, Ronan—I think it was a reaction after the accident, and perhaps the alcohol made me too impulsive.'

'For goodness' sake, Lisa, it was wonderful…' He looked down at her with laughter in his eyes. 'Don't tell me you didn't enjoy it—because I know you did. Anyway, perhaps I frightened you, taking things too quickly.'

She'd frightened herself, thought Lisa, terrified that, having fallen for the man, she would be hurt in the end by rejection. Just because she'd fancied him like mad at the end of a fraught evening, she'd compromised herself and made a working situation awkward. Anyway, she thought flatly, Ronan didn't want someone like her… She gazed ahead silently as they drove through the village, furious with herself for jeopardising a job she was enjoying.

When they got to the cottage Lisa almost leapt out of the car and ran down the little path, jamming the key in the lock to make her farewell as swift as possible.

From behind her Ronan caught her arm and looked down at her searchingly. 'You'll be OK?'

She pulled her arm away and their eyes locked momentarily, his compelling, hers embarrassed. 'Of course I'll be fine… Oh, and thank you for your help with my things. I'll go and sort everything out now and then have a good sleep.'

'We must have a meal again some time—and hopefully it won't involve a medical emergency!'

Lisa shook her head and said firmly, 'It was a lovely place for a meal, Ronan, but perhaps it would be wiser not to make it a regular thing…' She gave a short laugh to lighten her remark. 'A strictly working friendship is better, don't you think?'

'Ah,' he replied sardonically. 'So we'd better keep friendship and work separate, then?'

Lisa looked at him rather uncertainly. Was that what she'd meant? Then she turned and opened her front door, saying gaily, 'See you next week at work!'

She went inside and closed the door, leaning against it for a minute with her eyes closed. She was truly alone at last! Not living with anyone else, beholden to no one else and free to lead a new life as she chose—hadn't that been what she'd longed for over the past few months? She went to the window and watched Ronan's tall figure walk slowly back to his car before he drove back up the bumpy lane. She felt a lump come to her throat. It was so unfair! The one thing she hadn't bargained on was falling in love so quickly!

Ronan drove back slowly, replaying the bitter-sweet memory of the night he'd made love to Lisa. When he reached the house he sat for a moment in the car, frowning into the evening light. What was it with Lisa? he asked himself in a bewildered way. She was trying so hard to distance herself from him, obviously regretting every moment of that evening, and yet he knew that when they were together sparks flew. She couldn't have pretended that passion she'd shown that night. The fact was that Lisa was a knockout—feisty, gorgeous and fun—and it had taken him by surprise. He hadn't expected he could fall for anyone so quickly, but he had to be careful— Lisa wasn't about to commit herself to anyone in a hurry. He got out of the car and slammed the door in irritation. It was perfectly obvious that she had been hurt by someone in Grangeford and hadn't got over it yet. Someday, he promised himself, he'd find out the truth about Lisa's past.

For the next few weeks Lisa buried herself in her work, enjoying getting to know her patients, going on long walks at the end of the day, and revelling in the beauty of the scenery. Often her neighbour Mary would have a barbecue by the shore and invite Lisa along. She felt she was gradually becoming part of the community. But always at the back of her mind was an awareness of Ronan, a self-consciousness when she was with him at work—and incredible longing to be with him when she was alone.

Sometimes Ronan had come up to her after surgery and suggested they have a working lunch together to discuss various patients and future practice policy. At the end of their first meeting he had asked her to go to a concert with him at Inverleith and she had decided to be blunt with him.

'That's very kind, Ronan, but I think it would be easier if we had a strictly professional relationship from now on. It…it makes things easier, doesn't it?'

'If that's how you want it,' he replied casually. 'I guess we can still be friends, though?'

'Of course. I just don't want to make any more…mistakes, that's all.'

By which she'd meant, reflected Ronan, that she regarded the night they'd made love as a terrible error.

One Friday morning Lisa's mobile rang as she parked her car at the surgery. It was Lorainne.

'Hi, Lisa—Lorainne here. Thought I'd try and catch you before you started work. Just confirming that you'll be able to help out tomorrow at the coffee morning we're holding at Glenside House—Richard Carstairs's home.'

Lisa bit her lip and scrabbled for her diary in her handbag. It had been weeks ago and she'd almost forgotten her promise to help. 'Good job you rang me to remind me. Of course I'm coming—what time do you want me there?'

'About ten o'clock if you can—I expect people will begin coming about half an hour later. It'll give us time to set out cups and saucers and get the water heated.'

'I'll be there,' declared Lisa. 'By the way, good news on Harry, isn't it?'

'Yes, thank God. I thought he'd be in ICU much longer, but they moved him to a main ward and he made such good progress they allowed him home last week. Anyway, look forward to seeing you tomorrow. Be prepared for some long-winded speeches—Richard Carstairs sometimes gets carried away, but his heart's in the right place!'

'I'll be interested to meet him,' said Lisa. And that was an understatement, she reflected as she walked into The Coppice. She couldn't wait to meet a member of the family that had shaped her mother's life so drastically—not to mention seeing the house that had been so much part of her mother's childhood.

The waiting room was full as usual, a small battle seemingly taking place in the middle of the floor between three or four young children whose mothers were ineffectually trying to pull them apart, while a baby wailed in the background. Lisa made her way around them and joined Val, Cora and Ronan in the office.

'Surgery's very busy today Lisa,' said Val. 'I can't hear myself speak for the row!'

An especially loud shriek from the waiting room made Ronan put his hands over his ears. 'Sounds like a zoo,' he commented. He peered at the computer screen. 'First on your list, Lisa, is Tom Lachlan—you may find him a challenge!'

'How come?' asked Lisa, picking up a sheaf of e-mails with blood-test results on them.

'He thinks he knows better than any doctor, that's why,' said Ronan gloomily, taking a draught of coffee from a cup Cora handed him. 'And he won't be too pleased if you tell him he was nothing to worry about either—because he loves a good worry!'

'I'd better make a start, then,' said Lisa. 'Did you say we were having a practice meeting later?'

Ronan nodded. 'Yes, we'll meet in the room we use for the baby and diabetic clinics. Val will get us some sandwiches and I believe Terry will try and make it, especially now he knows Harry's out of danger.'

Lisa settled herself at her desk and pressed the button to call up her first patient. Tom Lachlan came in, a wiry little man with white hair and red cheeks, reminding Lisa irresistibly of an elderly elf. He sat down on the chair in front of her.

'I won't waste your time, Doctor,' he said without preamble. 'I know you medics have a lot of people to see, most of them complaining about nothing at all!'

'Then how can I help you, Mr Lachlan?' asked Lisa with a smile.

He folded his arms and pursed his lips. 'Well, I know what's wrong with me—I've got all the signs. It's an acute condition that flares up when I'm under the weather. I just need you to write a prescription.'

'I see—what is this acute condition?'

He thumped his chest melodramatically and coughed. 'There! Hear that? Rattling away something awful I am—almost certainly bronchitis.'

'Let me listen to your chest. Are you coughing a lot?'

'Oh, yes—whenever I thump my chest like that I start coughing. At night I can hardly sleep.'

Lisa lifted his shirt and vest and put her stethoscope on his back and then his front, listening carefully, then she tapped his chest with her fingers.

'What are you doing that for?' Tom asked curiously.

'The resonance of the sound this produces helps me to deduce the condition of your lungs—for example, whether you've got fluid in them or not.'

Tom pursed his lips and seemed to brace himself for bad news. 'So tell me the truth—is it bronchitis or pneumonia?'

'I'm pleased to say your chest sounds clear. You've probably had a cold and the catarrh has made your throat tickle,' she said.

Tom gazed at her in astonishment. 'What? You amaze me…can't you hear me wheezing?'

'No, I can't—everything seems quite clear,' she said. 'Do you smoke?'

'Look, Doctor, I don't want to be rude, but what's that got to do with it?'

Lisa put down her stethoscope on the desk and said mildly, 'Now, Mr Lachlan, don't tell me you don't know about the dangers of smoking—especially to your chest. A man of your intelligence? If you're coughing I think it's the effect of smoke in your lungs when you have a cold. I wouldn't want to give you antibiotics at the moment.'

The little man stood up angrily. 'So you're sending me away with nothing, are you?'

'Nothing except some good advice. Drink plenty of fluids, perhaps sip honey or blackcurrant juice with lemon —but don't smoke. I can guarantee that you'll feel much better in a few days.'

He picked up his cap, which he'd put on the desk, and pulled it onto his head. 'I doubt it,' he said shortly. 'I know what I've got—it's my body and I've read up all about the symptoms on the internet! Don't try and con me into thinking there's nothing wrong with me!'

He got up from the chair and stumped out crossly. Lisa

sighed. 'If you're not feeling better in a few days, come back and see me,' she said to his indignant back.

He turned at the door. 'Next time I shall probably go to Dr Gillespie,' he said with dignity. 'He usually backs up my diagnoses!'

Later, at the practice meeting, Ronan asked Lisa how she'd got on with Tom.

'He certainly prefers you to me,' she commented wryly. 'I think we're becoming a nation of self-diagnosticians. He seemed to know exactly what was wrong with him—and he wasn't pleased that I didn't agree with his diagnosis!'

'People read health articles in the press and on the internet and they're sure they've got symptoms they didn't know they had until they read about them!' remarked Ronan.

Everyone round the table nodded and Terry, who had limped in with two crutches, remarked, 'If you ask me, patients nowadays have expectations on which we can't always deliver. Everyone's an expert nowadays and advice isn't easily accepted. The patient knows best!'

'That's right.' Ronan grinned. 'Give me the old days any time when what the doctor said was gospel—I'm sick of all these opinions everyone has! And now let's get down to business. The first item on the agenda is the drug budget, then Rachel has some concerns about one or two of the elderly housebound patients, and finally I think Lisa has some points she'd like to raise.'

There was a lively discussion about the main points of the meeting, and Rachel told of her worries about the lack of sufficient carers for some of their more isolated housebound patients. Eventually they got down to Lisa's concerns.

'Don't tell us you're having second thoughts and want to

leave already, that you don't like us!' quipped Ronan. He smiled, the little white scar dimpling at the corner of his mouth, and his eyes held hers for a second as he said it.

Lisa swallowed, struck anew by how fantastic he looked when he smiled, and at this most inappropriate time in a practice meeting her mind was suddenly transported back to the night when they had made love. In her imagination she felt the touch of his mouth on hers, his hands exploring her body, how they had locked together in the most intimate of embraces. It was almost laughable that now they were sitting in a meeting and no one had an inkling of what had happened between them that night.

The people around the table were looking at her expectantly, and with a start she pulled herself back into the present, blushing at the thoughts that had been whirling around her head.

She took a deep breath and said, 'I know I've not been here long, but I think with a few simple changes we could easily change the layout and facilities in the waiting room—'

'What's wrong with it?' asked Ronan, frowning. 'It's got chairs and magazines. You don't want us to provide coffee, do you, or perhaps take down some of the walls?'

'You old reactionary,' chided Terry, grinning. 'Let's hear Lisa's ideas.'

'No, no, nothing like that,' said Lisa eagerly. 'When you came in here this morning, what struck you?'

'A hell of a lot of noise,' said Rachel. 'It was like a bear garden!'

'It always is,' agreed Cora. 'Whenever we have a full surgery it's like that.'

'It seems to me,' continued Lisa, 'that all the noise is caused by young children. If we gave them something to do, they might quieten down.'

'Parents don't seem to have any control over their offspring any more,' growled Terry. 'We ought to put up a notice, PLEASE RESTRAIN YOUR CHILDREN OR THEY WON'T BE SEEN!'

'What did you have in mind, Lisa?' asked Rachel.

'I thought we could make that small stockroom at the side of the waiting room into a play area—make it into a little house with a few toys and children's books. I'm sure it would help. I'd be willing to paint it. And there are other things, too,' Lisa said, now in the full flow of enthusiasm. 'We could have a book corner, not just magazines…'

'A what? We're not a public library, you know,' reproved Ronan mildly.

'No, honestly, I think a soothing comforting read would be a great thing—some surgeries even have poetry leaflets with well-known poems in them that can calm worried patients.'

'Could lower their blood pressure!' suggested Rachel. 'I think it's a great idea.'

Ronan looked at Lisa's animated face, how her large hazel eyes sparkled as she explained her suggestions, her face alight with enthusiasm. He sighed. She looked so beautiful, so lively and intelligent—no wonder he couldn't get her out of his mind. He frowned, trying to concentrate on the matter in hand.

'Where would you put the stock?' he asked. 'There isn't much room anywhere else.'

'This place is far too small, that's the trouble,' grumbled Terry. 'We'll have to extend or move—that's the bottom line, I suppose.'

'We could partition off one of the large surgeries and put

the stock there,' Lisa suggested. 'It wouldn't be very expensive, even if it was a temporary measure, and I'm sure it would help, especially when we have baby or diabetic clinics and mothers have to bring young children with them.' She looked around the table and smiled. 'Come on, it's not so revolutionary and it wouldn't cost much.'

Terry laughed. 'I suppose not. We are behind the times somewhat. Ronan and I were thinking of making changes before my accident, but the state and age of this surgery made us feel it wasn't worth it.'

'I suppose we should go for it,' said Ronan. 'I don't mind pitching in to help with decorating and putting up shelves…'

'If we made it into a little playhouse, I could make the curtains,' said Val enthusiastically. 'I think it would be a great idea—anything to keep the noise level down!'

'Perhaps we could make a start next week on Sunday afternoon? And then,' added Lisa mischievously, 'I propose to make a start on the little garden at the front of the house. I could soon jazz it up with a few plants…'

Everyone laughed and began to move out of the room, except Rachel, who was reading through the notes of patients she had to see, and Ronan.

'See you tomorrow at this wretched coffee morning, then,' said Terry. 'I've got to take the money, so I'll be stuck there quite a while, I suppose.'

He went out carefully on his crutches, and Ronan turned to Lisa.

'Can I give you a lift tomorrow?' he asked.

'Thanks, but I'll walk to the house from the cottage and go through the wood along the shore—it will do me good.'

'Well, just remember, I'm there if you need me, now you've moved to the cottage.'

She stood there stiffly, intensely aware of him, so close she could smell the faint tang after aftershave on him, see the dark flecks in his blue eyes. She let her glance wander over his narrow intelligent face and mobile sexy mouth. For a brief second their gazes collided and the electricity between them was like a flicker of lightning and she longed for nothing more than to feel his arms round her again.

'See you tomorrow,' she said brightly.

'Sure.' He strode out of the room, the smile fading from his face. They'd agreed to be good friends. He gave a short mirthless laugh. Good friends be damned—he wanted more than that, but for some reason she wouldn't allow him to cross that line.

Rachel was finishing the last of the sandwiches and biscuits from lunch as she looked over her notes. She looked up guiltily at Lisa. 'I shouldn't be eating these, I know,' she sighed. 'I'm horribly overweight—gone way over my calorie count for today, and here I am advising some of our patients to go on diets!'

'I find it hard to go on diets, too,' remarked Lisa, picking up her briefcase.

'You've no need to,' said Rachel gloomily. She looked at Lisa quizzically. 'You going to the coffee morning, then?'

'Yes, I've said I'll help.'

Rachel stood up and leant against the desk, her eyes twinkling. 'And Ronan's going, too? That's nice.'

Lisa looked at her sharply. 'What do you mean?'

'Oh, nothing… It's just that I didn't think he liked these interminable coffee mornings. I'm surprised, that's all. He must have had some incentive.'

She looked meaningfully at Lisa, an enigmatic smile on her face. 'Now, don't look so disapproving,' she added.

She ducked and laughed as Lisa threw a pencil at her, then went out of the room, taking the last biscuit with her.

CHAPTER EIGHT

So this was the house her mother had talked of, where she had lived so happily as a child until she'd been sixteen... Lisa stood at the entrance of the huge hall of Glenside House and looked round silently for a minute, taking in the beautiful staircase that divided halfway up and curved round to a gallery. A small dome in the ceiling high above had stained glass in it, and the light shining through split into coloured rays. Lisa could almost picture a little girl sliding down the curving bannister with shrieks of delight, followed by other young members of the family. Through the huge arched windows on the side wall one could see the park stretching out and the tree-lined drive up to the house. It must have been a magical place to have spent a childhood.

Lisa turned towards the bustle that was going on before her, with numerous people scurrying about, putting up trestle tables and carrying large trays full of crockery across the floor. On one table a huge selection of home-made cakes was displayed and Lisa could see Lorainne stacking cups and saucers by two immense tea urns. Someone had opened the large doors that led onto a terrace and small tables were being put up outside with chairs around them.

'What can I do?' Lisa asked Lorainne. 'Everyone seems to have a job!'

Lorainne grinned at her. 'Thanks so much for coming, Lisa—and don't worry, I've got the very job for you—selling raffle tickets. As the GP for most of the people round here, they won't dare refuse you!' She handed Lisa a huge bundle of tickets and pointed to a little stage by the staircase. 'All the prizes are on there—from pots of home-made jam to an old set of bagpipes for some lucky household! All you have to do is wander around, persuading everyone to buy tickets.'

'I'd better get going if you want me to sell all these. Which is Richard Carstairs, by the way?'

'I'll introduce you right now,' declared Lorainne, putting the last cup in its place. 'He's talking to Terry by the big doors—preparing to make his speech, I shouldn't wonder.'

She led Lisa across the floor to where Terry was sitting at a table, taking the entrance money from visitors. Beside him was a tall, distinguished-looking man with thick russet-coloured hair and dressed immaculately in a blazer and cream trousers. It gave her quite a jolt to think that this good-looking man was probably a relative of hers.

'Richard, can I introduce you to Terry and Ronan's new partner—Lisa Balfour? She's very kindly agreed to sell the raffle tickets.'

Richard smiled pleasantly. 'Great to meet you,' he said, offering his hand to her. 'It's about time Ronan had someone to help him. I do hope you'll enjoy yourself in Arrandale.'

What would her mother have said if she'd known her daughter was shaking hands with a Carstairs, was actually in his house, reflected Lisa. But, then, she thought with surprise, Richard Carstairs was so far in looks and manner from what she'd imagined a Carstairs would be like—a kindly open face and courteous manner, that she felt almost guilty about having imagined a kind of ogre.

'I think it's a beautiful part of the world—quite different from where I lived before,' she replied.

'And where was that?' he enquired.

'Grangeford…a very crowded city, almost under the runway of the local airport.'

'Well, I'm glad you've decided to settle here. I'd like you to meet my wife, Gill. She's around here somewhere—probably trying to control the kids.' He looked around the room and waved an arm at a woman near the tea urn with a baby in her arms and two small children clinging onto her skirt. 'Over here, darling! Someone I'd like you to meet.'

Gill Carstairs was plump, pretty and refreshingly down to earth. 'Isn't this a scrum?' she declared as she came up to them. 'You must be Lisa Balfour,' she added, smiling at Lisa. 'Mary Lovat's told me all about you and I was hoping you'd be here. It's lovely to have new people in a small place like this. Do take the children, Richard, while I do my bit at the stalls.'

Obediently Richard took the baby and bent down to kiss the other two. 'You come with me, troops,' he said.

'I see they've roped you in to sell raffle tickets—ghastly job!' Gill put her hand on her husband's arm before he moved away. 'Richard, I hope you're going to fork out for some!'

'Of course…of course. Give me ten books.'

'That's very generous…'

'Not at all. We all want the nursing home refurbished—it's a good cause. Now, your colleague, Ronan, is joining us for lunch on the terrace, so you must come too—mustn't she, Gill?'

'Of course,' said his wife. 'We must get to know our new doctor! See you later.'

Lisa watched them as they drifted over to the other side of the room. She couldn't believe how friendly and welcoming the Carstairs were, and suddenly the ghosts of her mother's past began to fade. They were nothing like the people she had described from her youth—the present-day Carstairs were lovely, and it wasn't Richard's fault that his grandfather had been an autocratic bully. She smiled to herself. Without diminishing what her mother had gone through, she was beginning to realise she could move on and not dwell on what had happened in the past in Arrandale any more.

She began to move through the crowd and several people bought tickets from her. She landed up near Lorainne, who was grappling with one of the tea urns, which was making an ominous hissing sound as she was about to open the tap for the water to go into large jugs.

'I hate doing this. I always think the thing's going to blow up,' she said, hopping back in alarm as the boiler started to spit boiling water out of the pipe.

'Allow me,' said a familiar voice. Ronan stepped forward from behind Lisa and opened the tap gingerly, holding the jug underneath as boiling water sputtered out. 'There you are,' he said with triumph, 'A skill born of long years in the Scouts! What else can I do?'

'You can go around with Lisa and help her sell raffle tickets—you can do the introductions and she can win them over to spend!'

'Fine by me,' he said quietly. He flicked a look of dry amusement at Lisa. 'I'm sure we'll work well together…'

A little shock of alarm went through Lisa. It had been a few weeks since they'd seen each other away from the working life of the surgery and somehow the atmosphere was very different—more relaxed, more intimate. The rules, she thought wryly, were very blurred when one wasn't at work. He took some raffle tickets from her and led the way through the crowd, and Lisa felt that delicious and dangerous flicker of attraction that crackled through her whenever he was near. He looked even more heart-stoppingly good-looking than usual—coolly casual and sexy in an open-necked shirt over a tanned neck and long legs in faded jeans. He was, Lisa reflected as she followed in his wake, by far the most attractive man in the room!

They came to a small knot of women by the cake stall, and he smiled at them.

'I'm sure these ladies will help us out. I think they're all patients of ours!'

Lisa watched how the women flocked round to buy tickets, calling out, 'Hello, Dr Gillespie, that physio you made me do really helped,' or, 'I'm feeling so much better since I saw you last month and you put me on those pills.', 'Glad that bump on your head healed up after the accident…'

'You've certainly got a fan club,' she said to him in amusement.

He looked at her sardonically, those amazing blue eyes burning into hers. 'Not everyone's so bowled over by me, Lisa,' he said softly.

Lisa swallowed hard. Over the past month she had tried to play it cool, doing her best to prevent any occasion they might meet at work being turned into anything personal. He probably thought she actually disliked him when, of course, all the time she longed and longed to be with him, do things with him. But it would be madness, wouldn't it? She'd learnt before that one couldn't mix romance and business, and she'd come dangerously close to that with Ronan.

A bell rang and Richard stood on the stairs above the crowd, a benign smile on his face.

'Just a few words, everyone. As you know, we're gathered here today to raise money for Corrie House Nursing Home. The council doesn't want to spend any more money on it, and if they don't the place won't come up to the required standard, so drink lots of coffee, buy as many cakes as you can—and also raffle tickets!' He waved towards Lisa. 'Our new doctor, Lisa Balfour, has plenty to sell so, please, help her out!'

He continued talking for a while, about the special debt their community owed to its old people and how convenient Corrie House was to Arrandale, then he wound up by flinging his arms open and saying expansively, 'Now, let the day begin—go ahead, Piper Cameron!'

On the terrace the drone of the bagpipes was heard, gathering pace into a lively tune, and a large man in a kilt and full regalia began pacing up and down outside.

Ronan laughed. 'Richard certainly is a showman,' he observed. 'I'm surprised he's not got Highland dancers on display in here!' He looked down at Lisa. 'So what do you think of your long lost relative?'

'He seems a really nice guy—it's such a relief really,' confessed Lisa. 'I'm beginning to realise that whatever happened in the past wasn't his fault. It would be stupid to continue to feel bitter. It was a long time ago now.'

Ronan nodded. 'I'm glad you think that. After all, why make a new life in Arrandale and still feel resentful about what happened to your mother? As you say, it's over and done with now.'

It was a good feeling, thought Lisa. For so long she had felt a bitterness towards the family she'd never met, forgetting that time had passed and the generation now was very different to their forebears. With a sudden lifting of her spirits she reflected that now she was going to enjoy Arrandale without any reservations about the Carstairs and hopefully become integrated into the little community. She flicked a quick glance at Ronan. The only fly in the ointment now was her relationship with him. She would have to try and lighten up and be more natural with him to keep their working life happy. She loved Arrandale and she enjoyed working at the practice—she'd just have to keep her true feelings for Ronan under wraps.

'You look very upbeat,' remarked Ronan, his glance taking in her sudden happy smile and relaxed manner. 'Richard's impressed you, hasn't he? Will you tell him you're a long-lost cousin?'

'Some day I will,' she replied. 'There's no hurry—I'll choose my moment.'

The morning went very well, with a huge crowd of people jostling through the house and spilling onto the lawns outside where further stalls were selling a variety of local produce and home-made goods. Lisa guessed that there weren't too many social occasions in an area like this, and everyone wanted to be involved. She and Ronan sold all their tickets, and just as they were taking their final bag of money to the central desk a small man came up to her. It was Tom Lachlan, the man who'd diagnosed himself as having bronchitis.

'Ah—hello, there, Dr Balfour. I'm glad I saw you.'

Lisa blinked. She hadn't expected such a pleasant greeting from the man after their last meeting in the surgery. 'Mr Lachlan… Er…how is the cough?'

'I owe you an apology, Doctor. It's completely gone—and do you know what I put it down to?'

'I can't guess!'

'Your tip on drinking honey and lemon juice. I added a good slug of whisky with it to make it more palatable. I have a large glass every four hours, and I've never felt so good in my life!'

The little man marched off and Lisa and Ronan looked at each other then burst into laughter. Ronan chuckled. 'I should think he's in an alcoholic haze. I'm surprised he managed to get here.'

Lisa giggled. 'I didn't know he was going to add extra ingredients, for heaven's sake!'

'It's certainly put him in a better frame of mind anyway—and surely that's a result for someone like Tom!'

And suddenly the atmosphere between them seemed so light, so much more normal. Ronan grinned down at her. 'I'll send all my awkward patients to you now,' he remarked.

'Don't you dare,' she said with mock severity.

'Lunchtime!' declared Richard Carstairs coming up to them. 'It's a lovely day, so we may as well be outside—this way. Bring Lisa along, Ronan.'

Ronan took Lisa's arm in a proprietorial way and shepherded her through the crowd. This time she didn't draw away. Lorainne and Terry were already sitting down under an umbrella and there was a huge bowl of salad on the table as well as platters of smoked salmon, prawns and cold ham. Richard placed Lisa between himself and Ronan, then uncorked a bottle of champagne that had been on ice. The atmosphere was relaxed and jolly and the setting idyllic with the happy sound of people chatting and laughing around them.

Lisa sat in the chair with her head resting on the back and through half-closed eyes covertly watched Ronan talking to the others. She took a deep sip of the champagne, wrinkling her nose as the sparkles exploded in her mouth, a slight dizziness making her feel muzzy—probably drinking on an empty stomach, she thought. She'd hoped as the weeks had gone by that she could cope with her feelings for Ronan—but she had been wrong. She fancied him more than ever. When they'd laughed together just now she'd been reminded of his sense of fun and how easy it was to get on with him. She closed her eyes and tried to blot out his image from her mind.

She jumped slightly when she heard Richard's voice in her ear, her eyes opening wide. He was waving a champagne bottle over her glass. 'A top-up for you?'

'No, thanks. It's delicious, but I think I've had enough.'

'Well, then.' He smiled. 'At least have something to eat— you haven't even started yet.'

He pushed some laden plates towards her, but for some reason at the sight of all that food she didn't feel hungry, a slight feeling of nausea floating through her.

Richard took some food for himself and settled back in his chair. 'I believe that at your interview you weren't too well— yet you kept going until you fainted?' he remarked. 'Brave girl indeed. Are you OK now?'

'Yes, I'm fine, thanks. Still the odd twinge, but I recovered very quickly.'

The irony was that her stomach was definitely 'off' at the moment. It was probably because she hadn't had any breakfast. Lisa nibbled cautiously at a piece of bread, hoping that would settle the queasiness.

Now it was getting late and people were beginning to pack

up the stalls and clear away the lunch tables. Lisa was surprised at how tired she felt. After all, she'd only sold some raffle tickets and been sitting down for lunch most of the time. She almost wished she hadn't arranged to go with everyone to transform the surgery stock room into a children's area the next day—she could do with a whole day off.

She rose to leave, and for a brief moment had a horrible feeling she was going to faint. It was definitely time to go home!

When Lisa got to the surgery the next day to start work on redecorating the stockroom, Ronan was already there. He'd spread dustsheets over the carpets and had started stripping the walls of their dirty yellow wallpaper. He was standing on a ladder, stretching up to strip the paper from the corners. His T-shirt had parted from his jeans and revealed a tanned muscular flat stomach, and he looked incredibly sexy.

'You're here early,' she said, looking hastily away from his athletic figure. 'Where are the others?'

He grinned down at her. 'I told them not to come. I said I'd do the basic painting first.'

'Oh…I see,' she said, rather taken aback.

So there were just the two of them, she thought, a mixture of alarm and excitement making her heart flutter slightly. An afternoon alone with Ronan had not been part of her plan.

'I wanted to make a good start,' Ronan said cheerfully. 'Put the kettle on, will you? I need an injection of caffeine into my system if I'm to keep going.'

Lisa went obediently into the office and filled the kettle. Her hands trembled slightly. It seemed so quiet in the normally noisy surgery, somehow giving an intimate atmosphere… She spooned some coffee into a jug and stared out of the window, her thoughts in a jumble. She was trying her best to keep Ronan at arm's length, but here, on their own together? He came down the ladder, wiping his hands on his jeans, and threw the scraper onto the floor. She handed him a mug of coffee.

He took a sip and grimaced at the taste. 'Sorry, I need a bit of sugar in this.'

He came nearer and reached around her to put two hefty spoonfuls in his mug, brushing against her arm as he did so. Lisa felt her insides melt slightly, every hair prickling on the nape of her neck He stood in front of her—rather too closely, thought Lisa nervously, and folded his arms as if about to make a statement, leaning casually back against the worktop.

They were so close they were almost hip to hip, his breath warm on her cheek—any nearer and that muscled leg of his would be pressed against hers. She backed away slightly, her senses as taught as a violin string, every nerve end in her body longing for his physical touch. His eyes held her gaze intently and she knew that he was going to say something that had nothing to do with work.

'I've been hoping we'd be alone for a while, Lisa,' he said softly. 'We never seem to get time to talk by ourselves.'

'It's very busy at work—is there something bothering you?' Lisa's mouth was dry and the words came out rather huskily.

'Well…since you ask…' He took a sip of coffee, watching her over the rim of the mug. 'I get the feeling you're keeping me at a distance.'

'It's what we agreed,' she replied quickly. 'We said we'd be friends.'

A quirky little smile lifted his lips. 'I know what we said, but it hasn't worked like that, has it? Friends are relaxed with each other, they do things together, laugh together. We don't do that.'

'Don't be silly…' Her voice was breathless. 'I look on you merely as a…colleague. We agreed it would be silly to be anything else. Not,' she added hastily, 'that there is anything between us, of course…'

'I don't believe you, Lisa.' He put a finger under her chin and lifted her face towards his, so that she could not avoid the gaze of those intense eyes. 'You know very well fireworks go off inside us when we see each other—ever since that night when—'

She put her hand up hastily. 'Stop right there! I've apologised for that. I led you on because I was shocked after the accident for one thing. Oh, and for lots of other reasons.' She was almost gabbling, her words tumbling over each other. 'But it's much better this way, maintaining a friendly professional relationship—surely you can see that?'

He looked down at her sternly. 'Lisa Balfour, for a month now I've tried to maintain a "friendly professional relationship", as you put it—but I may as well have been exchanging views with a wooden post for all the feedback I've had. I don't want that kind of association. I need more than that professionally…or otherwise.'

Lisa's heartbeat accelerated uncomfortably. 'I will try, Ronan. I admit I've been a little…frosty perhaps.'

He put his hands on her shoulders and looked down at her with flinty blue eyes. 'Yesterday at the coffee morning I began to feel that a few defences had come down. There was a hint of what it should be like between us normally. Didn't you feel that?'

His touch on her shoulders sent her heart clattering uncomfortably against her ribs. 'Perhaps,' she murmured cautiously.

His hands pulled her nearer, dangerously near again. 'Just what's bugging you, Lisa? We're free agents—neither of us are beholden to anyone. What harm really is there in having what I might call a "loving friendship"?'

'Ronan…we're on quicksands here,' she whispered. 'It would be wrong…'

'Why the hell would it be wrong? The trouble is that you're looking backwards all the time. Something happened to you in Grangeford and it's affected your life here.' His hands went around her waist and he drew her to him, murmuring in her ear, 'I don't care if we do work together. I can't for the life of me think there's anything wrong in doing this, and I know that you feel something for me, too—so what's frightening you?'

So much for willpower, Lisa thought distractedly as he took her face in his hands and brushed her lips with delicate butterfly kisses, then more passionately teased them apart so that despite herself she responded. Then his hands entwined in her hair and he trailed his mouth down her jawline to the little hollow in her neck, so that delicious sensations flooded through her entire body. In answer she wound her arms around his neck, pressing her soft contours to his hard frame. Every erogenous zone in her body reacted like a spreading fire.

Any minute now, she thought giddily, she would throw in the towel completely, allow him to make love to her on the surgery floor if necessary! An unexpected well of laughter surged through her as she pictured the scene. What did it matter after all?

Then gradually a warning voice started to sound louder and

louder in her head. How easy it would be to capitulate, to give herself as she had to Trevor. Had she learned nothing from her experience with him? In the end he had come to dominate her completely so that she had no longer been her own woman. She had lost that precious independence her mother had always told her to value—and she could not allow that to happen again. She pulled herself slightly away from Ronan, turning her face to the side and tensing her body.

Ronan opened his eyes and looked down at her, pulling her face back so that she had to meet his gaze.

'What is it, Lisa? You're doing it again, aren't you—leading me on one minute, then pushing me away the next?' There was a sadness in his voice and Lisa felt guilty, guilty because she had responded so eagerly to him.

'For a while I could swear you were enjoying yourself just then. It's not just my imagination,' he added softly. 'You and I are like positive and negative charges. Sparks fly between us when we're together—you know that!'

She wanted to cry, Yes! Yes, you're right! But something restrained her. 'I…I don't know what you mean,' she muttered feebly.

'Come off it,' he said scornfully. 'I'm not such a fool I can't tell that there was someone else on your mind besides me. Who is he, this man that has the power to intrude on our lovemaking, forces you to think of him and not me?'

Lisa stared at him, his stark words hanging in the air, shocking her into silence. He was right—Trevor still controlled her feelings as if he were still around, although she hadn't seen him for a long time. She dropped her eyes.

'What is it, Lisa? What on earth's bothering you? For God's sake, tell me!'

Lisa sighed and leant against the table. 'You're right,' she murmured dully. 'I haven't been able to get rid of my past, and it's not fair on you.'

He tilted her face to his and said more gently, his blue eyes softer, 'Please, Lisa, don't imprison yourself in things you've left behind. Tell me everything. After all, I've told you my sad little story!'

He looked around the small room and made an impatient gesture. 'Look, it's a lovely day. Why don't we forget the decorating in this airless place and go for a walk along the loch? And you can tell me everything. It might seem easier in the open air!'

She nodded. 'Perhaps you're right,' she murmured.

'Come on, let's go!' said Ronan, starting to stride out, his long legs covering the ground at a good pace.

It was quite exhilarating, with the slight breeze whipping colour into their cheeks and the cool fresh air from the mountains filling their lungs. Little waves whipped up on the empty shingle, and Ronan had let Tam out of the car so that he bounded joyously in front of them. Although Lisa felt revitalised out in the open air, she found it difficult to keep up with Ronan but was determined not to show how very unfit she was. He flicked an amused glance at her.

'OK? Not going too fast for you?'

'Of course not,' she panted. 'I'm enjoying it—just a little out of condition, that's all. I don't seem to have had time for much exercise during the last few months.'

Ronan slowed down his pace to a gentle stroll and took off his jacket, slinging it over his shoulders. It was getting very warm.

'I'm not surprised. You had a sick mother and a busy work life, didn't you?' he remarked.

'Yes…the last thing on my mind was keeping fit.'

'Then tell me about work first—it was a large practice, I believe.'

'There were five partners—one of them was my best friend. She and I were at med school together,' she began.

'That must have been pleasant, having a good friend as a colleague.'

She shrugged. 'It was—at first…'

'What do you mean?'

Lisa began to walk more quickly, as if that would help in the telling of the story.

'Sally Merchant was my friend, and her brother happened to be the senior practice partner—his name was Trevor. He was very attractive.' Her voice was flat, unemotional.

Ronan smiled slightly. 'I'm getting the picture,' he murmured.

'Sounds a good recipe for romance, doesn't it?' she said bitterly. 'Girl falls for best friend's brother at work? It didn't work out like that, though.' Suddenly she turned to Ronan with a distressed expression. 'Quite honestly, I feel it's nobody's business but mine!'

Ronan's smile became grim. 'Excuse me,' he said, holding her arm and pulling her round to face him, 'when the past involves how you feel about me, when something has happened to upset you, then it is damn well my business.'

The wind was whipping Lisa's hair against her face, and her eyes sparked defiantly at him. 'I don't know if I want to go on with this conversation after all,' she said tersely.

He held both her arms tightly so that she was unable to turn away from him. 'A few weeks ago we made love—wonderful, passionate love,' he rasped. 'Then suddenly it was as if you didn't want to know any more. What are you afraid of telling me, Lisa? What could possibly be so bad?'

She twisted herself out of his grasp and said as evenly as she could, 'I apologized, didn't I? I've admitted it was all my fault—I let myself get carried away. I…I didn't want to get involved again.'

He lifted an eyebrow. 'Again?' He kicked a stone moodily in front of him, then said brusquely, 'You know what I think? They say that sometimes the past can hold you back, but if you confront it then you can move forward—am I right?'

'Something like that, I suppose,' she admitted. She looked up at him and said almost pleadingly, 'I'm more wary of forming relationships now—but, then, I'm sure you are, too, Ronan, after your experience.'

He smiled wryly. 'That's true. But I've told you my background—it's your turn to tell me yours. There's no one else listening except the loch and the mountains!'

He pulled her down next to him onto a large piece of driftwood, and she looked across the white-flecked water and sighed. She couldn't go on denying her past. Ronan was right—she owed him an explanation.

She said slowly. 'I fell for Trevor in a big way. He was good-looking, fun and charming, and I suppose I was flattered by his attention. It was lovely to have someone looking after me while my mother was ill. I began to rely on him.'

'So what went wrong?'

'Gradually I began to realise that he wasn't the lovable man I'd thought. Underneath the charm and sex appeal he was arrogant and a complete control freak—as long as people agreed with him and did what he told them, he was OK. But when he was crossed—boy! He was like a Rottweiler. He began to dominate me completely, dictating what I should and should not do.'

She was silent for a moment, and Ronan prompted her quietly, 'Go on—tell me all.'

'It could have been a very happy arrangement,' Lisa went on. 'And I really wanted it to work. Sally would have been a lovely sister-in-law.'

'But?' interjected Ronan.

'You try working with an opinionated bully!' said Lisa simply. 'Eventually I couldn't cope with his attitude any more and I tried to finish with him.' She gave a short laugh. 'He refused to believe that I didn't want to go out with him. He was convinced I was mad about him really. I don't think he could imagine a woman not falling at his feet.'

'So what did you do?'

Lisa shrugged. 'It was difficult. We worked in the same practice, his sister was my friend and delighted that Trevor and I were dating.'

'I can see it would have been awkward,' agreed Ronan.

She was silent, looking at the shingle, kicking the stones with her feet.

'And that's all? Is that why you left?'

'It came to a head one evening.' she said at last. 'Stupidly I had a row with him after work about his unwillingness to take on elderly patients who would inevitably demand extra medical care—he raised the roof!'

'And then?' prompted Ronan.

Absent-mindedly Lisa skimmed a stone across the water and watched the rings as it landed, then she said slowly. 'Then I told him that it was final—I no longer wanted to go out with him, that I couldn't take being controlled and manipulated by him. It was awful. Everyone else had gone home—we were alone.'

Her voice trembled and Ronan gripped her hand. 'Go on, Lisa, tell me what happened.'

She swallowed and continued. 'He went kind of demented, saying I'd lied to him, saying I'd wanted to get engaged and he should have guessed what I'd be like…'

'Did you promise to get engaged?'

'Before I knew what he was really like, when I was still in love with him, yes,' she admitted. Her voice dropped to a whisper so that Ronan had to bend his head to hear her. 'He said he'd have to teach me a lesson and switched off the light. It was dark except for the light from a streetlamp and it made him look so eerie, so different.' She took a deep breath, as if bracing herself to continue. 'Then he tried to rape me—told me he'd show me what I'd be missing… He shook me, tried to hit me in the face…'

Ronan stared at her in horror. 'He what? God! What a bloody swine,' he spat out, his eyes flinty with anger.

'He'd never done anything like that before—nothing violent. Can you imagine the shock? I was stunned—I didn't even like him any more, but I'd never thought of him as an uncontrollable savage.' She shook her head in bewilderment. 'Can you believe that I could totally misread a person's character like that?'

Ronan gave a short bitter laugh. 'Yes,' he said. 'As a matter of fact, I can. As you've heard from my story, it's easy to get the wrong messages.'

His expression softened as he put an arm round her shoulders and hugged her comfortingly.

'So that was why you wanted to leave Grangeford so quickly,' he murmured.

'I did my best to fend him off, in fact,' continued Lisa. 'I'm glad to say I hit him very hard over the head with a paper-weight—that really hurt him. But if someone hadn't come back into the building at that point, I don't know what the outcome would have been.'

'You should have reported the man,' declared Ronan robustly. 'He deserves to be struck off the register.'

'Perhaps I should—it was horrible working with him after that. But I hoped he would behave himself, having nearly been caught in the act—and, of course, I love his sister. I felt it would drive a wedge between us if I said something—and I had no proof of what he'd tried to do. No one had seen us.'

'No wonder you wanted to leave the place,' commented Ronan drily. 'You were in an impossible situation.'

She looked up at Ronan, her large eyes holding his. 'Perhaps that's one of the reasons why I'm wary of having any entanglements when they're mixed up with work. If things don't work out, it's just intolerable.'

'We're not all potential rapists,' he said gently. He smiled at her and brushed the windswept tangle of hair back from her face. 'Now, you must draw a line under that part of your life—start again.'

'That's what I want to do,' she said firmly. 'And that's why I don't want to make any more mistakes…misread situations.'

'Sweetheart…' Ronan tilted her face up to his, and smiled into her eyes '…if you're too careful, you might miss the chance of happiness altogether—ever thought of that?'

Lisa bent down to pick up a stick and hurled it along the shoreline for Tam to retrieve. She watched him joyfully bounding after it then gave a sudden laugh. 'You're right—there's no point in wasting my life thinking about how Trevor treated me.'

He laughed with her and put his arms around her waist, lifting her up bodily and swinging her round. 'Alleluia! At last you've seen the light! Then can I take it you aren't going to allow that evil man to interfere with your thoughts when I'm kissing you?'

A sudden elation filled Lisa. Surely this time she could allow herself to love and know that in return she'd receive tenderness and kindness, not bullying and domination. Her smile was sweet and happy as she looked up at him.

'I shan't think of anyone else but you when we're kissing,' she promised.

He grinned, that sudden boyish grin that made him look much younger and softer. 'Then I take it, sweetheart, we can begin to enjoy life together with no, shall we say, inhibitions?'

In answer, she pressed herself against him and kissed him firmly on the lips.

With a shrill sound the bleeper on the jacket Ronan had slung over his shoulders began to go off insistently, making them both jump. Ronan pulled himself away from her with a groan.

'I thought it was too good to last. I'll have to answer that. I'm covering for the practice at Inverleith this Sunday.' He looked at her humorously. 'What a time to pick—I was just going to begin where we'd left off in the surgery!'

He stabbed out numbers on his mobile to the central medical office who co-ordinated on-call duties. 'Dr Gillespie here—you bleeped me. What's the problem?'

He listened intently to the information being relayed and made some notes on a pad. 'OK. Tell them I'll be there in twenty minutes and not to panic!'

Lisa looked at him questioningly. 'What's happened?'

'A woman staying at one of the more remote hunting

lodges has gone into labour, and there's been a landslide between her and the ambulance station at Inverleith. I've been asked to go along and assess her—they'll send a helicopter if I think it's necessary.' He made a face. 'It's been some time since I've delivered a baby…'

'I'll come with you—surely two of us can deliver a baby if it's a normal birth!'

CHAPTER NINE

THEY drove up through the spectacular forested glen, where great arches of trees met over the road like a green tunnel and buzzards wheeled overhead on the thermals. Lisa's heart sang because all at once she knew that things between her and Ronan had been straightened out. He hadn't actually said he loved her, but it was clear that he wanted her as much as she did him.

'Where is this hunting lodge?' she asked.

'Not far now—it's just off the road here and down an unmade track to a clearing. Apparently there's a small party of people staying there, probably for the fishing.'

'This woman couldn't have chosen a much more remote spot to have her baby,' remarked Lisa, hanging onto the dashboard as they bumped over the rutted track and parked in front of what looked like an enormous log cabin. An elderly man was pacing around outside, and when he saw Ronan and Lisa he almost ran towards them, an expression of great relief on his face.

'Thank God you've come! My daughter-in-law's started labour. She's very early—I told her not to come when it was so close to the due date, but she insisted.' He pressed a hand to his forehead. 'Oh, dear, I hope nothing goes wrong!'

Ronan put a reassuring hand on the man's arm. 'You just lead us to her and leave the worrying to us—what's your name, by the way?'

'Stuart—Kenneth Stuart. My daughter-in-law's name is Becky. She seems in terrible pain. I just wish her husband was here, but he and two friends went off at the crack of dawn to do some fishing, and I've no idea where he's gone. He won't know what's been happening. I feel completely helpless!'

'Has he not got a mobile number?'

'I've tried that, but the reception is very bad in the hills and there's no signal.'

'Not to worry, Mr Stuart. Listen, why don't you go and put on the kettle and we'll all have a cup of tea?'

Having given the distraught man something to do, Lisa and Ronan made their way upstairs to the bedroom where Becky was lying on a double bed, her hands above her head, clutching the spindles of the bedhead, her back arched. Every now and then she screamed, a high-pitched, frightened sound with the edge of panic in it.

Lisa went up to her and put a hand on her arm. 'Becky,' she said in a clear firm voice, 'don't worry now. I'm Lisa Balfour and this is Ronan Gillespie, doctors from Arrandale, and we're here to help you. I want you to try and relax while we see what's happening.'

The girl's scream tailed off and she looked at Lisa, whimpering slightly. 'I'm scared,' she whispered. 'I don't know what's happening, and it's so painful— Oh, my God!'

'It's all right, Becky, it's just a contraction—it'll be over in a minute,' soothed Lisa. 'Your body's doing its job, pushing the baby further down the birth canal. There, it's lessening now, isn't it? You're doing very well. How often are the pains coming?'

Lisa's encouraging words seemed to calm Becky, who clutched Lisa's hand in hers and tried to smile. 'I guess about every few minutes—it seems almost continuous! I never thought I'd be giving birth in the back of beyond like this...' she panted. 'I should be in London—that's where I'm booked in. I don't suppose I could be flown there...?'

'I don't think even if we were rocket-propelled we've time to get you there,' remarked Lisa with a grin. 'Now, let me just have a quick look to see if the baby's head's showing.'

She looked up at Ronan. 'She's in the second stage of labour—this is going to be fairly quick. I can see the crown of the baby's head already, and he or she's got blond hair! Now, this is where it's going to be hard work, Becky, but don't worry—everything's going very nicely. The baby's head's crowning.'

'Are you sure? Will the baby be all right? I'm at least three weeks early.'

'That's not too bad at all—the baby will probably be a very respectable weight.'

Becky looked tearfully at Lisa. 'We've waited years to have this baby and now that he's arriving the father isn't even going to see him being born! That's typical of Robert—never there when you need him!'

'Never mind—it'll be a nice surprise for him,' said Ronan with a smile.

Becky gave a sharp intake of breath. 'I'll give him nice surprise,' she muttered. Then she gripped the sheets. 'I want to push now! I can't stop!'

Ronan had put a sphygmomanometer around Becky's arm

and was monitoring her blood pressure. 'Can you pant for a minute?' he asked calmly. 'You're doing really well, but we want the baby to have a smooth passage out if possible. Well done! You're doing great!'

His eyes met Lisa's and he nodded. 'Now, put your head on your chest, Becky, and push for all you're worth... Terrific!'

Becky had forgotten to be frightened. She was really concentrating on pushing and then panting when instructed, gripping Lisa's hand in an iron grip. Then suddenly she gave a sharp gasp and within a few seconds a slippery little body, covered in blood and mucus, shot onto the towel that Ronan was holding. He massaged the baby's back for a second, holding the head down so that any mucus could escape, and then there was a lusty cry as the child took its first breath.

'Congratulations,' he said with a broad grin, holding up the baby for Becky to see. 'You have a handsome little boy...he'll be able to play rugby for Scotland!'

He handed the baby to Becky who cradled him in her arms, looking down at the child as if she couldn't believe her eyes. 'My little boy...my own little boy,' she murmured. 'I've waited such a long time for you!'

Lisa watched the little tableau with a lump in her throat, never failing to be moved by the arrival of a new human being to the world. 'What are you going to call him?' she asked Becky. 'Have you any names ready?'

'We'd thought about Callum—and now he's here, that seems to suit him, so Callum it is!'

'I've emptied a drawer, so I'll just put Callum in it for a minute while I tidy you up a bit—they're not very well equipped for newborn babies here,' said Lisa. 'Dr Gillespie's gone to phone the emergency services—I believe they'll be airlifting you out of here as they can't clear the landslide before tomorrow.'

Becky lay back on the pillows with a beatific smile on her face. 'I'm so happy,' she said simply. 'And I can't thank you and the other doctor enough. I think my father-in-law would have had a heart attack if he'd actually had to deliver the baby! And I can't wait to see Robert's face when he comes back!'

Ronan drove home slowly, both of them emotionally drained by the past hour and yet feeling a quiet elation in the happy outcome of the birth.

'One of the better aspects of the job,' murmured Ronan. 'Welcoming a healthy baby into the world.'

Lisa nodded, feeling a familiar wistful longing. Dare she imagine that one day she and Ronan would actually make a go of it and have children of their own? She gazed out of the window and a happy little smile curved her lips. Let's take things nice and slowly, she thought contentedly.

It was the end of a busy day. Lisa looked with distaste at the cup of coffee Val had put down on her desk. She didn't know if the twins were using an inferior brand of coffee or if they'd overboiled the water, but the smell made her feel quite sick. She popped another peppermint into her mouth to get rid of the taste. She'd seen the last patient of the day, thank goodness. She just had some paperwork to do and then she would go and have a quick nap at home before Ronan came to pick her up. They were going to have a light supper in the small bistro in Arrandale. He had said he had something he wanted to discuss with her and had refused to give her a clue as to what it was. Ronan and she had been together most evenings, and it was wonderful and exciting getting to know each other, giving the day a glow of happiness she hadn't felt for a long time.

She pulled the printouts of the day's e-mails out of the intray to look at the results of blood and ECG tests that had come from Inverleith Hospital, then looked up, startled, as a woman's loud voice floated through to her room. It sounded as if she was arguing, thought Lisa. Curious, she went to the door and peeped out into the corridor. A large woman was standing in the waiting room, her booming voice reverberating round the building.

'I've paid my taxes like everyone else,' she announced, wagging a finger at the twins, who stared back at her stolidly. 'And what's more I've given a large amount to that Corrie House Nursing Home appeal—even had one of the coffee mornings at my house. I think I'm entitled to a few favours even if the surgery is closing. For goodness' sake, it will only take a few minutes of the doctor's time.'

'Dr Gillespie's out at the moment,' explained Cora, her face pink with annoyance, although she spoke politely enough. 'Dr Balfour is just about to go home—she's had a very busy day, and you aren't a medical emergency.'

'How do you know that, pray—are you a doctor? Let's leave that sort of conclusion to the experts. I happened to be passing. I live a long way from the surgery and I have an extremely painful elbow. To come all the way here tomorrow would be incredibly inconvenient. I think if you tell the doctor that Mrs Rutherford needs attention, she'll be only too pleased to see me. Dr Gillespie will have told her how hard I work for all the medical charities.'

Cora flicked a glance at Lisa, standing in the door of her

room, and sent her an embarrassed glance. 'It's really not in order...' she began firmly.

Lisa grinned to herself. In her new happy frame of mind she was ready to put herself out even for someone like Mrs Rutherford, of whom she'd never heard.

'It's OK, Cora, please, ask Mrs Rutherford to come in,' she said, reassuring the receptionist with a smile. 'I'll make an exception this time.'

The woman plodded in slowly and dropped down into the chair. 'I thought you'd see me, Doctor, when you realised who I was,' she said complacently.

Lisa marvelled at the high opinion the woman had of herself. 'I happen to have a very full list tomorrow, Mrs Rutherford,' she said smoothly. 'It wouldn't have been possible to see you then anyway—unless you had something very serious. What is it that's worrying you?'

Mrs Rutherford leant forward in her chair, her protruding eyes like green marbles. 'For several weeks now I've had this terrible pain in my elbow. I'm in agony! I can hardly pick anything up—playing tennis is impossible!'

It was hard to imagine Mrs Rutherford playing tennis, but Lisa nodded gravely. 'If you've had this condition for some time, why didn't you come and see me earlier?' she enquired mildly.

The older woman drew herself up proudly. 'I'm a very busy woman, Doctor,' she said reproachfully. 'I can't just drop everything and come miles into Arrandale like some people can. But now I really need to see you because I've tennis matches coming up, and I need to be available.'

'Let me look at your elbow,' said Lisa, suppressing a smile at the thought of her forceful patient playing competitively.

She pressed the elbow gently, noting which part made Mrs Rutherford wince. 'Yes...this seems to be epicondylitis, or tennis elbow,' Lisa confirmed. 'You've an inflamation of the tendon that attaches the extensor muscles to the humerus.'

Mrs Rutherford made a tutting sound. 'And the receptionist said it wasn't serious! It sounds pretty serious to me. What's the treatment?'

'You'll have to rest your arm for at least two weeks—there are various treatments, but it does take a notoriously long time to cure sometimes. You could try anti-inflammatory drugs for a start, ultrasound treatment may help, and if the pain's persistent we could inject a cortisteroid drug.'

'A steroid?' Mrs. Rutherford shuddered. 'I don't think so—I don't want to look like a weightlifter, do I?'

Lisa smiled. 'I assure you, it won't have that effect, Mrs Rutherford.'

'Well, then, I suppose I'd better try the first option for a while.' Mrs Rutherford rose from her chair with some difficulty. Then with a surprisingly bright smile she said, 'Kind of you to see me, Doctor. I know how some people waste your time with apparent emergencies, so naturally you're chary of seeing just anybody at the last moment.'

'If it doesn't improve, do make an appointment to see me again,' said Lisa, slightly stressing the words 'make an appointment'.

Mrs Rutherford swept graciously out, and Lisa looked after her wonderingly. Talk about self-confidence and thick skin! Ah, well, she thought, switching off the computer and picking up her handbag, that's the beauty of general practice, you never know who'll you see next and with what complaint!

* * *

The bistro was crowded with a jolly atmosphere, and Monsieur Albert, the owner, bustled forward to show Lisa and Ronan to their seats in the window.

'There!' He beamed, throwing out his arm expansively. 'I hope you will be comfortable here. It is quite a secluded spot—what you need after the busy day in the surgery, *non*? Now you can discuss your medicine together in peace!'

Ronan grinned at Lisa. 'That's the last thing I'm going to discuss,' he murmured. 'I should think you've had enough of medicine today yourself, haven't you?'

Lisa giggled and told him about Mrs Rutherford. 'She seemed to think you would have mentioned her to me. Apparently she supports lots of charities…'

He groaned. 'She's rather a powerful character, I have to say, but if she takes something on she gives it her all. I can imagine she's the lynchpin of the tennis team!'

'I'd rather have her on my side any time,' commented Lisa, grinning at him. 'This is a really lovely place, Ronan. Arrandale seems to have quite a few good eating places.'

He looked at her profile as she gazed around the room, his eyes sweeping over her face, the slight blush on her skin and the arc of thick lashes shadowing her cheeks. At last, he thought, we seem to be on the same wavelength. He'd been beginning to think that this gorgeous woman would never admit that she was attracted to him—and no wonder she was scared after the terrible experience she'd had in her last practice. He leant forward and brushed her cheek with his finger.

'A penny for your thoughts,' he teased.

'I'm just thinking how happy I am—at last. I feel that

Grangeford was in another life—and so are the memories. I really feel I can move forward now.'

Their eyes locked for a moment and he said softly, 'I'm glad, sweetheart. Let's have a bit of fun, you and I. And that's what I wanted to have a word with you about.'

She looked at him, her eyes wide with interest. 'Hurry up, then! I'm dying to know what's on your mind. I've been thinking about it all day—don't keep me waiting!'

'First things first. Let's order our food…'

'Ronan! I'm not doing anything until you tell me what this is all about.'

He put his hands up, laughing. 'OK, OK, I'll tell you. The thing is, I'm due some time off and Terry is starting back full time next week. He suggested I have a short holiday—he doesn't mind holding the fort.'

'Where will you go?' asked Lisa, feeling a little flat. She'd thought it would be something that might include her!

'I thought of going to see Tanya in Italy, near Lucca—it's very beautiful around there. But I'll only go on one condition.'

'And what's that?'

'That you go with me!'

Lisa stared at him in amazement. 'With me? But what about the practice—how will Terry cope by himself?'

'A friend of his will come and do a week's locum work while he's up in this area. He's been attending a conference in Glasgow. It would be a great opportunity for us to have some time together,' Ronan added persuasively. He put his hand over hers at the table. 'Do say you'll come…a holiday would do us both good.'

'It sounds wonderful,' breathed Lisa, her eyes shining. 'Too good to be true. I haven't had a holiday for years, what

with my mother and moving. And if it could be arranged—
yes! I'd love to come.' She thought for a moment and said cautiously. 'What about Terry—won't he think it's strange, me
going away with you?'

'Does it matter that he knows? I should think he'll be delighted. As their daughter said, Lorainne's always on the look
out for a woman for me!'

'Even so, let's keep it to ourselves for just a little longer—
until we've made the arrangements?'

Everything seemed to have happened so quickly since
Ronan and she had unravelled their differences. She wanted
to hug her happiness to herself for a while before anyone else
knew they were an item. Ronan hadn't actually said he loved
her yet, but he was committed enough to want to go on holiday with her—and that was a start.

As if reading her thoughts, he smiled and said softly, 'We'll
take it slowly, sweetheart. Neither of us want to make any mistakes this time.'

No, they'd both had bad experiences and hopefully they'd
learned from them. Lisa leant back in her chair and thought
happily that everything seemed to be going perfectly. There
was so much to look forward to.

'Will we stay with Tanya?' she asked eagerly, remembering the attractive girl she'd first seen in the hospital after her
appendicitis operation.

'I think her flat's too small, but she knows of a lovely little hotel nearby and I know she'd love to show us around.'

It seemed too marvellous to be true. Lisa clasped her hands
together and sighed. 'I just can't believe this is happening. I
shall go and find the best that Arrandale has to offer in holiday attire!'

Ronan's eyes danced at her. 'I'd have thought you'd have to look pretty hard—but whatever you wear you look good in to me! And now, for goodness' sake, let's order some food. I'm starving, having spent most of the afternoon doing home visits in the depths of the hills.'

As they were having their coffee he produced some brochures about Lucca and the beautiful surrounding Tuscan countryside.

'It looks perfect, doesn't it?' He smiled, watching her face.

'Perfect,' she breathed.

He cupped her chin in his hand and gazed at her with a kind of amused tenderness. 'You know, Lisa, a few months ago when you came for your interview, I wasn't looking for a special relationship—that was the last thing on my mind. It didn't take long for me to realise—probably about three minutes—that I fancied you like crazy!'

Lisa grinned. 'It took me twice as long to realise you were drop-dead gorgeous!' She closed her eyes for a moment, savouring her happiness. 'You'd better pinch me and tell me I'm not dreaming!' She laughed.

Ronan had a word with Terry about the holiday and told him that Lisa would be going, too, if Terry could manage with his locum friend for a week. About to enter Terry's room one day for a meeting with a drug rep, Lisa could hear the two men talking and Terry's voice, rather loud and hearty floated, out through the door. She stopped for a second, realising that they were talking about her.

'I'm so glad that you and Lisa have hit it off. Lorainne and I think she's super—just right for you.'

'She's wonderful,' Lisa heard Ronan say. 'But we don't

want to rush things. It's taken some time to reach this stage and now we both need a holiday. Lisa would rather it was kept quiet for a little while.'

'Of course you both need to get away. You've borne the brunt of the work long enough while I've been off. And you and Lisa are made for each other…' Lisa heard Terry's deep chuckle. 'Thank God you managed to escape from that ghastly Maisie character. I still can't believe how she tried to land you in her net—totally untrustworthy!'

Other people began to come down the corridor and Lisa opened the door and went in, the rep following close on her heels.

It was late. Lisa had slept through the alarm and only been woken by the children next door shouting and laughing as they'd started off for school. She leapt out of bed and flung the curtains open, dazzled for a moment by the sun sparkling on the loch in front of her. As seemed so often the case, she didn't feel like breakfast but she forced herself to have a piece of toast and some weak tea, then flung herself under the shower before she went to work.

She sang happily as the cool needles of water hit her body. She and Ronan had had a wonderful evening, discussing the week they would have with Tanya and the trips they would take from her flat in Lucca when they took their holiday. Things seemed to have turned round so quickly between them in the last few weeks and she couldn't wait for them to go away together.

As she dashed out to the car she saw Mary standing by her window and gave her a merry wave, thinking briefly to herself that she looked as pale as a ghost, and that she hadn't seen her out and about for some time.

A sudden urge to vomit came over her suddenly without any warning. She grasped the roof of the car then somehow managed to duck behind the bonnet away from Mary's gaze. As discreetly as possible she bent down and got rid of her breakfast, then opened the door and slumped into her seat.

'What the hell's the matter with me?' she groaned. 'It can't be anything to do with my appendicitis—I recovered well from that. Why can't I eat, and why do I spend my time feeling like a wet rag?'

She slipped the car into gear and drove slowly to the surgery despite being late, her thoughts in a turmoil. When she got to The Coppice Val met her with a lugubrious face.

'The computer's crashed,' she said dolefully. 'I'll have to get everyone's notes manually from the shelves—and worse than that, Rachel slammed the door on her finger as she was taking the children to school. She's in agony but will be along in a minute.'

Lisa nodded rather absently, murmuring that she'd look at the finger when the practice nurse came in, then went to the toilet near her room. With trembling hands she opened her medical bag, drawing out a small cardboard box.

'You little fool,' she whispered as she opened it up. 'Why didn't it occur to you that this might happen?'

As if mesmerized, she watched the stick she had dipped into the tube from the box change colour. She stared at it for a few seconds, then drew in her breath sharply.

'Oh, my God...I'm pregnant! How on earth did that happen?'

She looked at her white face in the mirror over the hand-basin and grimaced. 'As a doctor, Lisa Balfour, no prizes for knowing what caused it!'

CHAPTER TEN

LISA ran the cold tap in the basin and splashed her face with water to try and bring some colour back into her cheeks. Her mind raced back to the evening of the accident and the passionate love-making she and Ronan had indulged in that night. She'd been so tired, so wretchedly shocked by the events of the evening that taking birth-control precautions had been the last thing on her mind.

'Just one night!' she murmured incredulously, then she reflected wryly that she shouldn't be so astonished. It always seemed to be happening to her patients!

She sat down on a chair and closed her eyes, her emotions as scrambled as ingredients in a mixer. She'd always wanted children, but she'd begun to think that was an impossible dream as time had gone on and she had got older. A little rush of excitement went through her to think that she was carrying a baby, that she would be a mum and Ronan would be the dad! Then gradually her enthusiasm plummeted. It might not have the happy ending she was hoping for. Would Ronan think she'd become pregnant to trick him into a permanent relationship, just as Maisie had tried to do?

Dully she stared at the opposite wall as Ronan's recent

words came back to her. 'She used the oldest trick in the world to trap me…' Tears welled up in her eyes—this should have been the happiest of days, a reason to rejoice. Instead, she felt cold fingers of despair tearing her newfound happiness to shreds. Ronan hadn't said he loved her—hadn't spoken of their long-term future—she'd just assumed they were a permanent item. If she revealed that she was pregnant and they got married, she would always feel that he'd done it because he'd felt morally obliged to—not because he'd really wanted to.

'I've spoilt everything,' she whispered. 'Just as I thought I'd got things right.'

Miserably she picked up her things and went through to her room. The day that had started so happily had changed to one of sad resignation. She couldn't go through with the holiday now—she couldn't continue going out with Ronan. He would say he wanted the baby—and perhaps he really would—but did he really want to get married, to settle down with her for the rest of her life, or would he only be pretending?

Cora knocked on her door and came in. 'Rachel's here, Lisa,' she said. 'Would you be able to look at her finger now?'

Lisa took a deep breath and tried to make her voice as even as possible. 'Of course—tell her to come in.'

While Cora went to get the practice nurse Lisa quickly patted her eyes and put on some more lipstick. By the time they came back she was quite composed and smiled at them.

'What happened?' she asked the white-faced woman.

'I overslept,' Rachel said, grimacing as she nursed her hand. 'Then I tried to rush and didn't take enough care shutting the car door when I dropped the children off at school…I feel a real fool.'

'Let me see,' said Lisa. 'And you're not the only one who overslept—so did I!'

She took Rachel's hand and looked at the right index finger, already swollen with a purpling nail, and drew in a deep sympathetic breath. 'That looks extremely painful!' she exclaimed. 'A real beauty of a subungual haematoma.'

'When I do things I don't do them by halves,' admitted Rachel. She winced as Rachel touched it gently. 'Ouch! It's really throbbing. Can you do anything to relieve the pressure?'

'I certainly can.' She paused for a second then said briskly, 'Is Ronan in yet?'

'He's calling in to see one of his heart patients before he starts. He won't be long,' Cora informed her.

A feeling of relief swept over Lisa. She didn't want to see him just yet until she'd decided what she could do. She turned to Cora. 'Well, in that case, Cora, you'll have to help out here.'

A flicker of horror went over Cora's face. 'What, me? Oh, dear, I can't stand the sight of blood.'

Lisa smiled. 'It's all right, we're not doing brain surgery here. All I want you to do is hold Rachel's finger while I puncture the nail.'

Cora looked even more alarmed. 'What will you do it with? A knife?'

Even Rachel laughed. 'Hopefully she's not going to cut off the whole finger…just a tiny hole to let the blood escape.'

Nervously Cora took Rachel's hand and Lisa put the tip of a pin into the flame of the little gas ring by the sink.

'Those who can't watch, look out of the window now,' she instructed.

Very firmly she pressed the sterilised pintip into the fingernail, and with the tiniest puff of smoke a hole was made through the nail and a small spot of blood oozed through it.

'Oh, my God!' squeaked Cora. 'It's worked!' She sat down suddenly on the chair next to Rachel. 'I never thought I'd be performing surgery today.'

Rachel puffed out her cheeks as the colour returned to them. 'What a relief! It really was painful. Thanks so much, Lisa. I even think I could manage a few of those custard creams with some tea now!'

On cue, Val bustled into the room with cups of tea for Rachel and Lisa and overheard Rachel's remark. 'What about that diet we're supposed to be on, Rachel?' she said sternly. Then she turned to her sister. 'Cora, come here and help me to retrieve the patients' notes while the patient recovers—the whole thing's a nightmare. I've no idea of the patient timings—there'll be some arguments over whose turn it is, I'm sure…'

'What's going on?' Ronan popped his head round the door, and then came into the room and put down his bag, looking in concern at Rachel.

She held out her hand and showed him her blackened nail and he grimaced. 'Not very nice,' he murmured. 'Looks like you've had first aid on it already.'

'Lisa's just put me out of my misery—I slammed the car door on my finger. Am I grateful to her—she did it so quickly and I feel human again.'

He grinned at Lisa, his eyes caressing hers in an intimate glance. 'Top marks to Dr Balfour. It had to be done before the blood started to clot.'

Lisa wound a small gauze pad round the nail and avoided his glance. 'Just keep this on to protect it for a while,' she said briefly.

'Then if all's well, I'll make a start on my list now,' said Ronan, turning to Cora and Val. 'I hear that damned computer's crashed. You'd better get in touch with the IT company—it's going to be chaotic if we don't get it working soon.' He turned to Lisa and murmured, 'Can I meet you at lunchtime? I've had an e-mail from Tanya about hotels near Lucca, and we can discuss dates.'

Lisa sat down abruptly at her desk as everyone left the room and put her head in her hands. What was she going to do? She could almost anticipate Ronan's disbelief if she told him she was pregnant, his growing scepticism about the situation. After what he'd told her about Maisie, how could she expect him to be ecstatic? Wouldn't he just assume it was another sort of trap? Glumly she pressed the patient call button. She'd have to think of something to say before lunchtime came.

Mary wasn't well at all. Indeed, she looked as if she was going to faint. Beads of perspiration were on her brow and her eyes looked hollow, sunk into their sockets. Every now and then she gave a hoarse cough. Lisa took a quick assessing glance at her.

'How long have you been like this, Mary?' she asked.

'Over a week now—it's like flu. Just when I think I'm getting better, I seem to have a relapse. I'm supposed to be going on holiday in two days' time—first one we've had in three years. The kids are so much looking forward to it.'

She had another bout of coughing, wincing as she did so.

'I didn't think you looked too well this morning when I was going out to work. You should have told me, got Dan to come round. It would have saved you coming to the surgery.'

'I didn't want to bother you,' said Mary miserably. 'You looked in such a hurry.'

'I'd always come and see you, Mary. Anyway, let's try and sort you out. Does it hurt your chest when you cough?'

Mary nodded. 'It does—and when I breathe in. I've tried hot towels on my chest, breathing in vapour—none of it seems to work…'

Lisa listened carefully to Mary's chest, then tapped her fingers sharply on her back, pursing her lips as she concentrated.

'I can hear sounds that shouldn't be there,' she told Mary. 'You've obviously got a lung infection—a type of pneumonia—and that's what's making you feel so ill. I don't even need to take your temperature to know you're feverish.'

'What about the holiday?' asked the woman miserably.

'I don't think so. You're not well enough and it's going to take a good two weeks to get you right. I'm going to put you on antibiotics and I want you to have complete bedrest for a few days.'

Mary opened her mouth to protest, but Lisa was firm. 'If you don't do that, you'll get worse and may have to go to hospital. It's just not worth going away—you wouldn't enjoy it anyway. Is Dan here to take you back?'

Mary shook her head and Lisa stood up. 'Then I'm going to take you—you're the last patient this morning and it won't take me a minute. Here are the keys of my car—you know which is mine. Get in while I just finish a few notes and I'll be with you in a minute.'

The woman obviously felt too ill to argue and went out slowly, murmuring, 'Thank you Lisa, you're very kind.'

Lisa scribbled down the antibiotics she was prescribing for Mary—she would enter all the notes into the computer later when the thing was up and running. And perhaps when she had taken Mary home she could ring up Ronan at the surgery and say she was visiting a patient and wouldn't be able to meet him for lunch. Not, she thought wretchedly, that playing for time was going to change anything at all.

She managed to smile reassuringly at Mary a few minutes later. She was slumped in an exhausted fashion in the car.

'Right! Let's get you home pronto…and I shall be keeping an eye on you to see you don't get out of that bed until I say so!'

'I…I'm so grateful for the lift.' Mary looked at her anxiously. 'It's so lovely having you around and I hope you're enjoying working here. No regrets about joining the practice? Some of the locums Ronan's had while Terry was laid up haven't liked being in such a quiet spot.'

Lisa didn't answer, although she wanted to say, Don't worry, I love it here—I'd like to stay for ever and ever! But now the future was much more uncertain. Suddenly circumstances had changed and she'd have to reassess her plans.

Almost as soon as she'd dropped Mary at her cottage, Lisa's mobile rang. Reluctantly she picked it up, realising it was Ronan.

'Hello, Lisa!' His voice was jovial, happy. 'Where are you? Don't forget we're meeting to discuss the holiday in about half an hour. Shall I get sandwiches in and we'll discuss things in my room, or do you want to nip out to a pub?'

She'd have to meet him—it was useless to put it off. 'I'll meet you at the Highlander's Arms in the village in ten minutes,' she said.

By the time she'd got to the pub Lisa's mind was made up. She would keep the news of her pregnancy to herself for a while and meanwhile make some excuse for not going on holiday—give herself a few weeks to come to terms with it herself. The truth was, she didn't know how Ronan would take the news and she was frightened—frightened that he'd think she'd deceived him. He'd made it clear that entrapment was not the way to a loving relationship, and perhaps he was right.

Ronan was standing by the bar, easy to spot as his impressive figure towered over everyone else waiting to be served. He saw Lisa come in and waved, pointing to a table in the corner for her to sit at. She shivered as she sat down, anything coherent flying out of her mind.

He carried two glasses back to the table and plonked them down. 'Only soft drinks, I'm afraid —we'd better not breathe alcohol fumes over the patients this afternoon.' He looked at her appraisingly. 'You look a bit peaky, sweetheart—have done for some time. I ought to give you a medical.'

'I'm all right,' she said hastily.

He eyed her doubtfully. 'You definitely need a holiday. Don't forget you've not really had any time off since your op.' He sat down and took a deep draught of his drink. 'I've ordered some ham sandwiches—hope that's OK?'

Lisa bit her lip…this was going to be so very difficult. 'I'm not terribly hungry, Ronan. I had a late breakfast. But I…I need to talk to you about the holiday.'

He smiled, that beautiful smile that softened his face, made him look less austere. 'That's why we're here, honey. Planning is almost the best part of it!'

She swallowed hard. 'The things is… The thing is,' she repeated desperately, 'I may need to revise my plans about going away.'

His happy expression changed and he frowned. 'What do you mean—revise your plans? Do you want to make it later in the year or something? We may not get a locum then, of course…'

'No…no, I just think it would be better if I didn't go with you at the moment.' Her words came out in a jumbled rush and he stared at her uncomprehendingly for a moment.

'What on earth are you talking about? You wanted to come— we were both looking forward to it. What's the problem?'

She was silent, unable to bring herself to articulate the real reason. 'No problem,' she whispered miserably. 'I just feel that now isn't the time for us to go together.'

He looked at her with almost comic bewilderment. 'I'm not with you. Why isn't it the time? For heaven's sake Lisa, we've been through all the rigmarole of our past mistakes. I thought we were all set for a bit of fun in our lives, time for ourselves together…'

'Time for ourselves together.' The words echoed dully in Lisa's mind. With a baby on the way there wouldn't be time for themselves—for evermore there would be someone else to consider and plan for…

Lisa stood up, feeling she just couldn't continue a conversation in which she was keeping things from Ronan—deceiving him.

'I'm sorry, Ronan, desperately sorry. I can't really go into all the reasons why I can't come with you. But I do think I'll take the two weeks off on my own anyway. Perhaps some time apart would be a good idea.'

Ronan jumped up, scraping his chair back noisily behind him so that several people looked round.

'I don't believe this—I can't understand what's brought it on. I was so sure that this time we'd sorted everything out.' He held her arms, and looked at her with burning blue eyes.

'It's my fault isn't it?' he rasped. 'I've rushed you—taken things too quickly. Is that the reason?'

Lisa squeezed back the tears that threatened to spill down her cheeks. 'Perhaps we have rushed things a little.' she said quickly, grasping at the reason he'd given. 'It's not long since Trevor and I finished and I don't…'

'Want to make the commitment?' supplied Ronan with an ironic smile.

He ran his hand in a distracted way through his thick hair so that it stood up in little peaks on his head. 'The thing is, Lisa,' he added bitterly, 'it's never going to be the right time, is it? I thought you'd put the episode with that man behind you—but I was wrong. You'll be thinking about it and using it as an excuse not to form another relationship for years to come!'

She could barely look at him. 'It's not that,' she choked. 'I need more space, that's all—more space to think things through.'

'Very well.' Ronan's voice was quiet. 'If that's what you want, have your space. But, frankly, if you don't feel enough about me now to know what you want, I doubt you ever will. I shall take two weeks' holiday alone next week. If you feel that working with me is going to be a problem after that then perhaps you'd better find somewhere more congenial.' He looked at her sadly. 'You see, sweetheart, I don't think I could stand to be so near you and not be part of your life.'

The waitress appeared with the sandwiches and put them on the table.

'Is that all right, sir?' she asked.

He brushed past her and strode out of the room, leaving Lisa staring in desolation after him.

* * *

That month the light stayed late in the Highlands, and the sky was still a duck-egg blue tinged with the pink of sunset at ten o'clock. It was an idyllic scene and yet Lisa was oblivious to the beauty in front of her as she sat outside her cottage in the balmy evening air. The same thoughts whirred round and round in her mind like a carousel—how much she had missed Ronan during the past several days, and had she been a complete idiot not to tell him about the pregnancy?

Then she thought of the reasons she hadn't told him—his wish to have time alone with her, his wariness of being trapped into a relationship… No, she'd been right to keep it to herself. OK—she would have to bring up a child on her own, be a single parent like her mother. But it could be done—indeed, she had her mother's example to follow. Unconsciously she tilted her chin. This child would never think it was unwanted—she would devote her life to giving it as good a start as she'd had without a father.

Running across the shingle and shrieking with laughter came the Lovat children, being chased by their father. They'd obviously been out somewhere. Mary was feeling much better now and she was following more slowly behind. She walked up to Lisa and flopped down on a garden seat next to her.

'Hi, Lisa,—isn't it a gorgeous evening? I'm still playing the invalid, I'm afraid, and persuaded Dan to take us out for a pizza this evening rather than cook.'

'The kids look as if they're enjoying themselves with Dan,' remarked Lisa, forcing a smile on her face.

'Yes, he's a great dad. I don't know what I would have done without him in the past couple of weeks since I've been ill. He's been a rock.'

Lisa watched Dan and the children disappear into their cottage. They were a lovely family, there for each other in good and bad times—just as the Newmans were. A sudden sob choked in her throat and, despite squeezing her eyes together as hard as she could, a tear rolled down her cheek. If she brought her child up on her own, she'd be denying it a family just as she had been denied one. She pulled a handkerchief out of her jeans pocket and blew her nose. She didn't realise that Mary had been watching her with some concern.

'What is it?' Mary asked softly. She put a hand on Lisa's arm. 'There's something wrong, isn't there? I've noticed that you've looked so sad these past couple of weeks—please, tell me.'

'It's nothing,' snuffled Lisa, more tears pouring down her cheek in a reaction to Mary's kind words.

'There obviously is something wrong—you don't cry for nothing.'

'I'm being a fool, Mary, only myself to blame. I've got myself into a muddle, and I think I've ruined my future!'

Mary looked at her in surprise. 'Surely it's not that bad, is it? Nothing that can't be fixed?'

Lisa gave a hollow laugh and twisted her hands together in distress. She flicked a look at Mary. She was a kind woman and they'd got to know each other quite well over the last few weeks. It would be a relief to tell someone about her dilemma—the stress of keeping things to herself was very hard to bear.

She gave a long drawn-out sigh, then the words came out in a rush. 'The thing is, I'm pregnant! And I don't think the father would react well to the news!'

Mary looked at her in astonishment for a second, then exclaimed, 'Pregnant? Oh, love, you poor thing—you've been keeping this to yourself for ages, haven't you?' She put her arms around Lisa and hugged her. 'I've been thinking you haven't looked very well these last few weeks—as a matter of fact, I saw you being sick behind the car the other day, although you ducked down.'

'I hoped you wouldn't see,' muttered Lisa.

Mary looked searchingly at Lisa. 'But you want the baby, don't you?'

'Of course. I've always longed to be a mum. I just didn't plan it very well! And me a doctor!' she joked weakly. 'I just don't think it's the right time for the father. He…he might not react well.'

'But you don't know that for sure, do you? To be honest, I think you ought to give the man a chance. He deserves to know the truth, your baby deserves a hands-on father if possible.'

'But an unwilling father?' Lisa looked at Mary wistfully. 'You see, I know he loves children, but he has had an experience before when a girlfriend told him she was pregnant. It was a lie, but it was an attempt to catch him. I would hate him to be pressured into commitment.'

Mary leant back on the garden bench and regarded Lisa sagely. 'You know, I think you do this man a disservice. I'm not completely blind—I have a pretty good idea who you're talking about. It's just got to be Ronan!'

'How did you know?' whispered Lisa.

Mary laughed. 'Not so difficult to guess—the way his eyes follow you about the place, the number of times he comes to the cottage. Good Lord, woman, all those evenings together can't just have been to discuss surgery matters!' She paused then and said slowly, 'I have noticed that he hasn't been around for a week or two, though.'

'He's on holiday—he went to Italy to see his sister. I was

going, too, but then I found out I was pregnant. Somehow I couldn't tell him—I just said it was better if I didn't go.'

'And how did he take that?'

Lisa shrugged her shoulders. 'Badly. He said I obviously couldn't make a commitment.' She turned to Mary. 'He said it was better if we parted—he virtually told me to look for another job. And he's right, of course, I can't continue working so close to him.'

'You love him, don't you?' said Mary gently.

'Yes,' whispered Lisa. 'But I refuse to send him down a road he may not want to go down. That's why I'm going for a locum position in a practice near Glasgow.'

'Think about it very carefully,' advised Mary as she got up. 'I think you ought to tell him—but, of course, it's your decision.'

Should she tell Ronan or not? Lisa still let the question hammer in her head long after Mary had gone. It was easy for Mary to be so positive, but to be manipulated into commitment was not a good basis for the future, reflected Lisa sadly.

Lisa knocked at Terry's door. It was the end of surgery and about time for the coffee-break the doctors took at that time. He looked up with a surprised smile as she came in.

'Hello, there! I thought you were to have two weeks off—you've got another few days to go. Couldn't keep away from us, is that it?'

'Just a quick word, Terry,' Lisa said. She sat down opposite him and smoothed her skirt nervously. 'I…I've got something to tell you—before Ronan gets back.'

Terry lifted his eyebrows enquiringly. 'What's up?'

'The fact is…' Lisa started off rather haltingly, then began to talk quickly, getting it over as quickly as possible. 'Well, o be honest, Ronan and I have had a bit of a falling-out. I know this is very sudden, but I've been thinking about things and I really feel that working closely with him would be very difficult. The long and short of it is that I've applied for a locum position near Glasgow.'

Terry looked at her in astonishment over his glasses, then took them off and got up and came round the desk. 'You've what? You must be joking. I thought Ronan and you were, well, getting on marvellously. I even said to him the other week how well suited you were to each other. And we all hoped,' he added gently, 'that you and he would get together permanently.'

'It's better this way,' said Lisa tersely. 'I'm sorry. I have enjoyed working here so much—lovely people, lovely area. I know there should be a certain amount of notice to work out, but in the circumstances I think Ronan will agree to my quick departure.' She put an envelope on the desk. 'Would you give that to him, Terry? I think he's due back in two days.'

Terry picked it up and put it in his jacket pocket. 'I'm very sad about this. Won't you consider waiting a little longer before you make your mind up?'

'I don't think so…best make a clean break. I'll speak to you again before I go.'

Her voice was clipped, mechanical. No good being emotional about things now she'd made up her mind. She turned and walked out briskly, leaving Terry scratching his head and wondering what on earth had caused the rift between the two of them.

Lisa threw the last of her clothes into her suitcase and fastened the belt round it. A mixture of sadness and fury filled her. She seemed to be constantly on the move, and this time

it was entirely her own fault. If only she'd been more careful... She gazed unseeingly in front of her, thinking about
what might have been, how much she missed Ronan and how
she would never, ever meet a man that she would love again
like him.

She glanced at her watch. It was 10 a.m. If she left now
she'd be at the new place by lunchtime without hurrying.
She'd already said her goodbyes to the women at the practice,
giving some lame excuse for leaving, saying she'd found it
quieter than she'd thought it would be. She wouldn't forget
their look of astonishment in a hurry. Then last night she'd
gone round to Mary's with the cottage key, asking her to keep
an eye on the place until she could sublet it.

'You're mad, Lisa,' Mary had said forcibly. 'Ronan will be
distraught when he finds out.'

'You're not to tell him why,' Lisa had replied fiercely. 'One
day I may tell him, but I need more time.'

'I'll not tell him you're pregnant,' Mary had promised.

A sudden banging on the front door almost made Lisa
drop the suitcases she'd just picked up.

'Damn,' she muttered. 'It's probably the postman.'

She opened the door and the light streamed in, making it
difficult for a minute to make out who the person was standing there.

'Why the hell didn't you tell me the truth?' rasped a deep
angry voice. 'I've only just realised what you've been keeping from me. How could you do this to me?'

Lisa stepped back in shock and Ronan pushed his way into
the cottage. They stood opposite each other, his clear blue eyes
boring into hers.

'What do you know?' she faltered. 'And how do you know it?'

Her heart hammered painfully against her ribs. He looked so marvellous, tanned by Italian sun, anger giving his strong face a vital, intense look.

'When I heard from Terry that you were leaving, I came round to find out where you were going. I saw Mary by her front door just now.'

'Did Mary tell you? She promised she wouldn't say—'

'She didn't tell me you were pregnant, if that's what you mean. She stopped me and told me that you've been off colour and sick. The way she told it, I began to put two and two together—I am a doctor, remember. I recalled how peaky you were looking on that day when we had lunch.'

He pulled Lisa down onto the settee beside him and said more gently, 'Why did you keep it from me? Do you know so little about me that you think I'd let you have this baby by yourself?'

'I...I thought maybe you'd feel trapped again after what Maisie did to you,' said Lisa, then added with more spirit, 'No good being forced into the role of fatherhood if you're not ready for it.'

Ronan ran his hands through his hair in frustration. 'Trapping me... You little fool, I want to be trapped by you, ensnared, captured—however you want to put it. And I don't want our child to be brought up without a father—a loving father.'

Lisa put her chin up defiantly. 'I'm perfectly capable of bringing up a child by myself. I had good training from my mother, even if it won't be brought up in the lap of luxury like you were!'

He grimaced. 'Oh, please! Don't give me that, sweetheart. Do you really want this baby—our baby—to only have one parent by choice? I don't believe you!'

She dropped her head, feeling suddenly ashamed and embarrassed, and whispered, 'Not by choice, no…'

Ronan turned her face towards him. 'And that was what all this was about was it? The reason you wouldn't come on holiday with me?' He looked grimly at the cases by the front door. 'And the reason you're going to Glasgow?'

His arms went round her body and pulled her close to him. 'You little fool,' he whispered. 'I can't wait for us to have this baby—to bring it up together. Can't you tell? I'm absolutely thrilled!'

A little balloon of happiness seem to explode somewhere in Lisa's head, and she laid her cheek against Ronan's rough chin. What, after all, had she been thinking of? How could she have imagined that Ronan would not have wanted to be involved any more with her because she was having his baby?

'If you're thrilled, so am I,' she murmured.

He looked down at her with a grin. 'So thrilled I can't wait to introduce my future bride to the rest of my family! It's time to meet your new mother-in-law, I think!'

And Lisa laughed. It was all so simple really!

EPILOGUE

THE light poured through the stained glass window in the chapel, bathing the couple in front of the altar in a rainbow of colours. A loud wail came from the child the minister was holding as he dripped the baptismal water on her head.

'Letting the old devil out!' exclaimed Cora. 'Poor little Rosie—it must be so cold, that water!'

The godmother handed the baby back to Lisa and both parents gazed in pride at the plump baby trying to pull Lisa's earrings from her ears.

'Rosie Celia Gillespie,' murmured Ronan. 'Our first daughter!'

Lisa looked at him impishly. 'Our first? How many were you thinking of?'

He grinned. 'Now I know how lovely it is to be a dad, I think we could have a few more, couldn't we?'

A look of sweet understanding flickered between them and Ronan bent to kiss Lisa's cheek. Then Lisa turned to Richard, one of the godparents.

'It's really kind of you to have offered the Glenside Chapel for the christening,' she said gratefully. 'It's made it so special for us.'

Richard stroked the baby's face and smiled. 'Now you've told me that Rosie's related to the Carstairs, is part of the family, it's only right she should be baptised here. Our children are thrilled they've got a new relative.'

'She's a lucky little girl to have so many relatives,' said Lisa.

Gill moved forward. 'Now, would everyone come through to the large hall?' she said brightly. 'Everything's ready for the christening lunch, so come and eat and drink Rosie's health.'

As the small crowd made their way from the chapel Lisa looked about her in wonderment. To think that her mother's granddaughter should be christened in the family home her mother had known as a child was almost like completing a circle, as if a line had been drawn under an unhappy past and in its place something fresh and exciting was growing.

She looked up at Ronan, her handsome and wonderful husband, hardly able to believe that their lives should have turned around so amazingly from unhappiness to joy.

There was a stream of the friends Lisa had made since she'd come to Arrandale, all longing to look at Rosie or hold her. Then Richard and Gill's children asked if Rosie could be put in the pram and pushed round the hall by them.

Lisa watched as the little group took turns in pushing the pram, before returning a gurgling Rosie back to them—and felt a lump come to her throat. How, she wondered, could she ever have contemplated bringing up Rosie on her own, denying her the pleasure of the wonderful ready-made family she had here in Arrandale? It felt so right that after a lifetime she and her daughter were in the place and with the people where she truly belonged.

'I'm so lucky,' she murmured to Ronan.

Ronan bent down and kissed first his daughter's forehead and then Lisa's. 'I'm the lucky one sweetheart,' he whispered.

MILLS & BOON®

Live the emotion

_Medical
romance™

NEEDED: FULL-TIME FATHER
by Carol Marinelli

The grand opening of Heatherton A&E doesn't quite go to plan, so nurse manager Madison Walsh must rely on, and trust, new consultant Guy Boyd to save the day. Trusting turns to loving, but Madison has her daughter's happiness to consider...

TELL ME YOU LOVE ME by Gill Sanderson

John Cameron is a loner, travelling the world as a professional diver. For reasons of his own he's wary of getting close to anyone – until he meets Dr Abbey Fraser. John instinctively knows he needs to be part of her life. Then they discover they share a secret...

THE SURGEON'S ENGAGEMENT WISH
by Alison Roberts

Nurse Beth Dawson has chosen small town life for some peace and quiet. The last person she expects to meet is Luke Savage, the high-flying surgeon she was once engaged to! Luke has changed, mellowed – realised what's important in life. But will he forgive Beth for leaving him?

***A&E DRAMA: Pulses are racing in these
fast-paced dramatic stories***

On sale 3rd February 2006

*Available at WHSmith, Tesco, ASDA, Borders, Eason,
Sainsbury's and most bookshops*

www.millsandboon.co.uk

MILLS & BOON®

Live the emotion

Medical
romance™

SHEIKH SURGEON *by Meredith Webber*

Dr Nell Warren fell madly in love with Sheikh Khalil al Kalada – but he could never be hers. Now Nell must journey to the oasis city where Kal is a successful surgeon. He is the only man who can save her son's life. Not because of his skill – but because he is Patrick's father…

THE DOCTOR'S COURAGEOUS BRIDE
by Dianne Drake

Dr Solange Léandre has dedicated her life to the rural clinic in Kijé island. When specialist Paul Killian visits, he's mesmerised by her. But how can this city doctor show Solange that he has the dedication for life in the jungle – and the passion to care for a strong-willed woman?

*24:7 Feel the heat – every hour…every minute…
every heartbeat*

THE EMERGENCY DOCTOR'S PROPOSAL
by Joanna Neil

Consultant Mark Ballard is challenging and demanding – yet somehow he awakens doctor Sarah Marshall's desires. As they work together, Sarah secretly hopes their professional respect will become personal. When she gets another job offer – from a former lover – it's time for Mark to take a stand!

On sale 3rd February 2006

*Available at WHSmith, Tesco, ASDA, Borders, Eason,
Sainsbury's and most bookshops*

www.millsandboon.co.uk

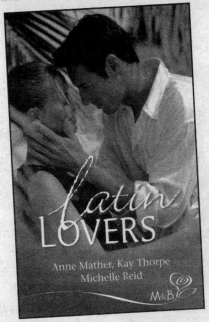

Three fabulous stories from popular authors Anne Mather, Kay Thorpe and Michelle Reid bring you passion, glamour and pulse-raising Latin rhythm and fire.

On sale 3rd February 2006

Available at WH Smith, Tesco, ASDA, Borders, Eason, Sainsbury's and all good paperback bookshops

www.millsandboon.co.uk

4 FREE

BOOKS AND A SURPRISE GIFT!

We would like to take this opportunity to thank you for reading this Mills & Boon® book by offering you the chance to take FOUR more specially selected titles from the Medical Romance™ series absolutely FREE! We're also making this offer to introduce you to the benefits of the Reader Service™—

- ★ FREE home delivery
- ★ FREE gifts and competitions
- ★ FREE monthly Newsletter
- ★ Exclusive Reader Service offers
- ★ Books available before they're in the shops

Accepting these FREE books and gift places you under no obligation to buy, you may cancel at any time, even after receiving your free shipment. Simply complete your details below and return the entire page to the address below. You don't even need a stamp!

YES! Please send me 4 free Medical Romance books and a surprise gift. I understand that unless you hear from me, I will receive 6 superb new titles every month for just £2.75 each, postage and packing free. I am under no obligation to purchase any books and may cancel my subscription at any time. The free books and gift will be mine to keep in any case.

M6ZED

Ms/Mrs/Miss/Mr ....Initials ....
                                                                              BLOCK CAPITALS PLEASE
Surname ....
Address ....

....

....Postcode..

Send this whole page to:
UK: FREEPOST CN81, Croydon, CR9 3WZ